THAT RESPLENDENT DAY

THAT RESPLENDENT DAY

A VISIONARY NOVEL BY

BRADLEY BERG

"The story is intriguing...the prose is insightful..."
Publishers Weekly/BookLife Prize Contest 2024

PALMETTO
PUBLISHING
Charleston, SC
www.PalmettoPublishing.com

Paperback ISBN: 9798822975903

eBook ISBN: 9798822975910

DEDICATION

This book is dedicated to all those who strive to serve the common good.

The Author is grateful to the following people for their role in helping to manifest this book; DK, MM, AAB, Arthur, Ben, Bill Luckey, Andrea K and Jan.

DAWN

Zeal arose from deep within Zune's soul
on this long-awaited day to resume his most special Journey;
I am ready, and the time is now.

CHAPTER 1

The Infinite Highway of Life has a relentless current all its own. One can enter and join its eternal flow. Destinations may be planned or unrevealed until one arrives. Successfully managing circumstances, our destiny can be created—sometimes alone, often with others; sometimes in action, perhaps in stillness.

Traveling this road, Zune rarely has much sense of time or how long he had been progressing along it. Maybe days at a time. Perhaps months, or even longer.

The last few weeks were spent letting go of whatever might have held him back from what he likes to call his Journey on the Infinite Highway. The gravity of attachments evaporated like dew on a cool, sunny summer morning. With his vision firmly set on his Journey into an unknown future, there were no anchors to deter him. Zune felt an incredible lightness in his soul.

Fully alert, exquisitely tuned to numerous impressions touching his five senses, his sixth sense, mind, was open yet still. Gone were the incessant ramblings of undirected mental activity. The stream of thoughts arising were only those he chose.

Zune's blue eyes, light-brown hair, slim build, and handsome face suggested a man in his prime. His fiery heart and strong hands revealed an amiable, magnetic nature. Some sensed a mysterious, timeless depth to his well-grounded presence.

Zune's hybrid, all-wheel drive, convertible car was tuned up and ready to go. Packing his chosen belongings in the trunk, he imagined his car was also psyched to hit the road, just as he was. His friends thought he was eccentric when they heard him talk nicely to his car, yet this was how he spoke to his dog, too, and they both sure seemed to respond well.

Some folks might have thought it strange for a man so content and well liked to just step out of his life, again, and drive off toward an adventure in the great unknown. For Zune, it wasn't about leaving things behind, nor was uncertainty a concern. He was moving forward into a future soon to be discovered and created. *It's not that something is missing; it's that something is possible,* he thought. Zune was utterly ready.

Leaning back against the car door, Zune slid a phone out of his front pocket to call his brother Kent. "Hey, bro. Just calling to let you know I'm about to get in the car and take off on the Journey."

"Gee, you really are going. Have a great trip!"

Zune appreciated that Kent shared in the excitement. "Thanks so much for taking my dog Molly, Kent."

"Sure, Zune. When will you be back? Last time, you were gone for almost two years," Kent wondered aloud.

"Well, since I'm heading out on the Infinite Highway, I don't really know." *He must realize by now this is way beyond just another road trip. I'm not sure if I really will ever be back.*

"Hey, if you can remember your high school Spanish, Zune, vaya con Dios."

"Yep—'Go with God.' Adios, Kent."

With that last bit of farewell, Zune hung up, checking over his car one last time. In the driver's seat, just before pushing the start button, a deep exhalation released everything in his psyche other than this moment.

As the car purred, Zune robustly voiced aloud his favorite lines from a poem by Walt Whitman:

"'Afoot and lighthearted, I take to the open road, healthy, free, the world before me, the long, brown path before me leading wherever I choose, Forever to know the universe itself as a road, as many roads, as roads for traveling souls, alive, forever forward. Strong and content, I travel the open road.'"

Turning onto his destined road, Zune felt a surge of joy vibrating within him. He welcomed the unknown challenges inevitably awaiting. The greater the obstacles overcome, the greater the reward. From effort we harvest increased strength and wisdom.

Zune tuned his satellite radio to smooth, up-tempo, instrumental jazz music, not wanting to hear a singer's lyrics interfere with his clear and open mind. In a few minutes, Zune was out of town, on the open road, warm wind through the windows gently blowing back his hair, eyes far ahead on the beckoning distance.

Cruising along for a while, Zune was outwardly focused only on his experience of richly adorned vistas, verdant hills, and open expanses. The scenery was singing to him. Radio off now, he hummed along to the silent, wordless music his lucid mind was creating.

Many hours—or maybe it was days—later, Zune was ready for a break. He began to keep his eyes peeled for the rare turnoff to a town. Eventually, he saw a sign—"Bleakville: one mile." Zune took the exit.

I sure hope they don't mean it's bleak here. Maybe that's just the name of someone named Bleak who founded this town. But given the old and ill-kempt-looking buildings coming into view, a faint, gnawing sense of bleakness arose within him.

Oh well, I just want to get some gas and something to drink. Maybe they have sparkling water with lime. If it doesn't feel right here, I don't need to stay.

CHAPTER 2

The radiant light of late afternoon sun illuminated the rocky summit of the Adirondack mountain peak rising proudly before her. Soft, welcoming earth gave way to stony terrain. The ascending trail spiraled above the thorny throes of life's everyday challenges into these majestic mountain moments Neeya so deeply treasured.

Striding more quickly now, her breath rapid and deep, Neeya grew strengthened as she approached the summit. Fatigue and aching legs didn't matter. Finally reaching her goal, she was richly vitalized. The awe-inspiring power of the mountain peak coursed through her veins, infusing her with its very nature. The wide-sweeping panorama revealed the expanse of nature's wonder.

Alone, yet a part of all she beheld, standing still between past and future, Neeya savored the exquisitely exhilarating clarity of the present moment. It was time to just be and feel it all. She remained in this state for almost an hour, the nebulous aspirations of her soul yearning to sing their song into manifestation.

As she turned toward the trail heading back down the mountain, Neeya avowed to hold on to the uplifting experience of the mountaintop. Yet as always, it slowly became increasingly elusive. Thoughts crept in, a mental gravity bringing her consciousness back down to the reality of a life waiting for her in the big city. She soon found herself becoming enveloped within a cocoon of thoughts about brother, lover, job, parched mouth, and tiring legs. Neeya purposefully shifted her full attention to the intricate colors, sounds, and aromas affirming the abundant life of nature surrounding her.

Not far from her car waiting below at the trailhead, Neeya slowly yielded to the pull of life in the civilized world, imagining herself as a successful international video journalist making documentaries about cutting-edge humanitarian issues like massive wildfires, war, or starvation. She would be there where it counted, revealing to the world how these crises impacted us all. It wasn't a vision of fame and fortune, though these briefly came to mind, but more a recognition by others of her real ability and her worth as a woman—a worth yet to be fully realized.

Neeya wondered if she could stomach another year as a paralegal for a law firm, engaged in tedious, mundane issues having no real significance for her. Stagnation was preventing her from reaching the level of fulfillment she sought. *I feel like my feet are stuck in the mud.*

Neeya paused beside a bubbling stream meandering through the thickly forested mountain slope, tumbling over rocks in its rush to join the river in the valley below. She considered her own life, meandering here and there, plowing ahead in a never-ending stream of redundant chapters, moving along of its own volition, bereft of self-determination. Pausing, Neeya let the stream's momentum flow through her toward a vague tomorrow. *Yeah, I'm flowing along the river of my life, but wow, it seems my boat needs a rudder. I sure don't seem to have much control. And that's just what I need to do—to steer things in a new direction.*

Watching the stream glide over smoothly worn rocks, she listened to its bubbling gurgles. Bending over the edge of the water, Neeya dipped her hands in, splashing her face, feeling the cool water refresh her, and yearning to sip from the stream to quench her thirst. Three thousand feet up the mountain, where the trail met the stream and the clear water looked so pristine, she knew even there, away from civilization, it was not a good idea to drink the water without boiling it. *Heck, I'd rather take one swallow from this stream, risking a bout of giardia, than to deny nature's offer and drink warm water from my plastic bottle.* Neeya cupped her hands, taking a slow, full swallow of the fresh, cool water, imagining it coursing through every cell in her body, becoming part of her, living within her.

Refreshed in soul, and now in body, Neeya was content for the hike to end. Reaching her car, she plopped down on the front seat. *Gee, I feel so tired, but it's that good kind of tired. My body is weary, but my head is clear. I really need to do this more often.* But then: *I hope Hank will come see me tonight.* Neeya knew even the presence of her boyfriend would somehow diminish the fullness of the mountain experience, as her focus would be on him. She and Hank had been together for almost three years. Sometimes she thought he loved her too much, though he was a source of comfort on which she could often depend. Neeya rhetorically wondered how she could have just let anything distract her from those wondrous moments alone in nature, feeling the fullness of her own being.

Neeya peacefully drove along the dirt road back toward the highway, passing low stone walls, lush, grassy meadows, goldenrod, and high-bush cranberry, standing tall. The streaming Native American flute on her car stereo felt perfect, allowing her to just listen, drive, and be.

Thoughts of her brother Favian came to mind. Neeya felt so close to him. They were best buddies growing up. Though their lives diverged when they left home after high school, the bond remained. Favian was always in her heart and mind. She envied her brother for having a mission and being able to really live it. He had an IT job for a small salary in an agency providing infrastructure development in Senegal, promoting local self-reliance and community resilience.

Neeya pictured him sitting on the hot ground, speaking in French and pieces of a local dialect. The work encouraged villagers to see the value of organizing and pooling their limited resources for farming. If they coordinated their efforts, instead of farming as separate families, they could grow enough staple food. *I sure hope he's okay.* She paid a lot of attention to current events around the world and knew from the emails Favian had sent that there was always a slight risk for an American there, even with a so-called charitable, nonprofit organization. There had been some civil strife in Senegal, and locals occasionally resented the intrusion of outsiders.

Her sister Angela was another matter. Angela was outwardly pleasant to her, but Neeya sensed it was all for show, seasoned with veiled insincerity. They were close growing up, but not like with Favian. Angela was always competitive and often critical.

Neeya noticed it was approaching six o'clock and easily gave in to the impulse to turn on the radio and catch the news. *Gee, I'm such a news junkie.*

Neeya quickly got bored listening to commercial, mainstream radio with only headline coverage about stories like industrial zoning issues in Albany and a triple murder in the Bronx. She tuned to a local FM college station in time to hear about food-insecure people rioting for lack of food in Haiti. Neeya became pensive as she listened to the journalist describe how Haiti once grew its own rice but now the tiny country was so poor it was desperate to get a loan from the World Bank. A billion dollars a year in US tax dollars was given to rice farmers in the US so they could sell food to Haiti for lower than it cost Haitians to grow and sell their own rice. Now, the cost of importing cheap rice had just tripled, and most people couldn't afford it. *So, the locals are going hungry while a handful of profitable Big-Ag businesses in the US are getting free money. There's something wrong with this picture.*

It unnerved Neeya to imagine that while she was listening to the radio in her comfortable, air-conditioned car, even with gasoline well over $6 per gallon, people were hungry and starving right off the coast of Florida. *In our own backyard. Something doesn't quite make sense. I want to be able to live my basic life without it negatively affecting people somewhere else.* Neeya wasn't sure if there was really such a thing as karma, but she was noticing how, in life, it sure seemed like what goes around comes around. It was bad enough to worry that some of her tax dollars went to wars which never ended, and maybe she helped pay for a hand grenade which accidentally blinded an eight-year-old girl who was in the wrong place at the wrong time. At moments like this, Neeya liked to imagine, *They will figure out a way to take care of all these major problems,* yet she wondered just who "they" really were.

Neeya was looking forward to stopping for two large slices of coal-fired pizza and a bottle of local craft beer at a cafe she liked to go to after hiking in the Adirondacks. However, the images of a crowd of people in Haiti rioting for food almost nixed her appetite. Neeya did stop for pizza, and it filled her empty stomach, though an uneasy feeling quietly lingered in her belly.

At home, drifting off to sleep that evening, images of Favian, Hank, and the people in Haiti merged with the exaltation of the hike up the mountain peak and the empty yearning for more out of life. Neeya eased into a dreamy mélange of a sleep which renewed body and brain yet left an indelible seed of discontent resting deep in her psyche—the kind of discontent which was healthy, impelling us to overcome the stagnation of a life unfulfilled, a life where real meaning manifests only when one harkens to the subtle call heard from within.

Neeya awoke to a sunny Saturday morning, glad to have the weekend to herself before going back to work. Barefoot, in a rusty-brown T-shirt and orange shorts, she stood before her bathroom mirror, brushing her shoulder-length brown hair with deliberate, slow strokes, big brown eyes peering into her own image. *It's sure worth it to have tired and achy legs from yesterday's hike. And it's so weird to have felt so exuberant, yet so unfulfilled. I need to figure out how to make some changes.*

After cooking breakfast, Neeya sat before the TV, watching her favorite streaming news stations. It was good to see some level of rebuilding in Ukraine, yet it left her so disturbed to see a country and its people ravaged by a war they never intended. It really bothered her to remember how a high school social studies teacher had said that the history of the world was the history of wars. *Can this really be such a messed-up planet?*

Neeya thought the intense friction and utter lack of bipartisanship displayed in the US Congress was a sorry reflection of unnecessary animosity and an unwillingness to compromise or cooperate. During the section about the troubled economy, she wondered, *Does it really matter if the stock exchange is still going straight down if half of*

Americans don't even have money to invest? Staring at massive plumes of smoke arising from fires in the Amazon, purposely set to clear land for crops to benefit the wealthiest farmers, she felt some relief knowing her hybrid car could get fifty-eight miles per gallon. A*t least that's one way I'll put less CO2 in the sky.*

Neeya reflected, *It's just so strange to feel hopeful, yet sad and worried about the world at the same time. Guess I'm pretty idealistic, but I wish I knew what I could do that could be helpful. At least Hank is coming over tomorrow and there's some time for laughs and intimacy.*

Neeya was still feeling physically spent that evening after yesterday's strenuous hike, especially after the long, busy days at work that past week. She was unmotivated to get undressed and ready for bed. Fatigue took over as she kicked off her slippers and lay down on her living room couch.

Neeya's eyelids lowered. Her attention withdrew from the external world. Sleep irresistibly beckoned ever so softly. Moments later, it was as if she was somewhere else.

In a round room with no ceiling, a soft, blue light filled the air, its hued mist veiling the faces and genders of those gathered together at a circular table. This group radiated an intense sense of power, yet it felt so very peaceful too. These were wise ones, considering matters of profound importance. *Maybe they are developing plans to help humanity solve our problems.* Neeya felt the scene's solemnity.

It was as if Neeya was present in the room with them, in the otherworldliness of the setting. She experienced a sense of safety and caring. Then a golden, glowing light emerged from the center of the group, raying forth as the whole scene dissolved.

Neeya awakened, feeling she had just experienced something real, leaving her with an undefinable, uplifting warmth. Whatever it was had touched her so very deeply. It was hard for Neeya to doubt there was something kind of spiritual about it.

Later, Neeya tried to inwardly deny she had been asleep and that it wasn't a dream, but she was unable to convince herself. *That could actually have been real, right?* The alternative was really too strange to consider, at least for now. Neeya recalled the Jedi Knights from the *Star Wars* movies with their use of the Force, quickly dismissing it as a silly comparison. Even so, she could still feel the benevolent, powerful presence of the group of wise ones, whoever or whatever they were. Maybe it really didn't matter, as the special warmth she still felt was real.

Early the next afternoon, Hank was there at her door. He strode up the steps and into Neeya's arms. It was comforting to feel his strong and affectionate embrace. He really loved her, and she was generally happy with him. Hank had recently been talking with her about living together. Neeya resisted, wanting to preserve the possibility of a path not yet clear or defined but free—free to be herself. Hank might be a bit of a deterrence.

Neeya thought, *Maybe I'll tell Hank about the dream*, but felt she needed more time to process it. After all, he was not the deepest kind of guy and would probably have no idea how to relate to it. *I can't risk letting him burst my bubble. I still feel the dream.*

Neeya's eyes shined a warm, early-evening softness, drawing him into her tender and receptive embrace. They enjoyed doing things together out in the world, but what she really liked about being with him was the cuddling and comfort she found there. He was so affectionate and unchallenging. His love for her flowed freely, and she absorbed it readily. Even so, Neeya was unsettled by a vague sense something was missing with Hank. She could let go of her cares and stress when there was just his smile and contagious laugh. He was content with life and had no motivation to grow, while she yearned for more meaning and a greater sense of worthiness in life.

Lately, being with him was just about the only time she really felt good. At times this was undermined by an awkward image of herself as an infant being comforted in her mother's arms. Her uneasiness faded as it was replaced by their shared physicality.

In the afterglow of their togetherness, Neeya lay there quietly as he slept, her weary mind now free to drift into abstract realms of imagination. She traveled to an impoverished, underdeveloped country to shoot a documentary about local villagers rebuilding their homes and schools after an earthquake. Her documentary was nominated for an award. These images sublimated into formless waves of dreamless sleep. On this night she found rest and in the morning awoke renewed.

From her apartment on Manhattan's upper west side, Neeya usually took the subway to her job as a paralegal in a law office near the corner of Fifty-Third Street and Broadway. On this day, however, Neeya was feeling good and decided to walk down Columbus Avenue, noticing her legs were still a bit achy from the mountain hike.

Neeya tried to like her job. The law firm which employed her provided defense attorneys, and she felt good to support their efforts to keep people out of jail, even if they were accused of white-collar crimes. She was aware that some of their clients really weren't so innocent and avoided these thoughts when confronted by them. That made life at work a little easier, though she often felt bored, lacking motivation.

"Good Monday morning, Neeya!" exclaimed her bright-eyed coworker, Kim. Neeya liked and respected Kim for her kindness and keen intellect. Her warm, upbeat greeting helped Neeya sustain a positive mood as she sat down at her desk with one too many files to go through today. By late morning, Neeya took a break and found Kim in the staff room drinking tea, working her way through a large chocolate croissant. Kim easily read the envious look in Neeya's eyes, and in a moment, Neeya was thanking her profusely for half of the delicious treat from a French bakery around the corner. "Kim, I sure owe you one for this!"

As they chatted, Neeya was surprised to hear Kim venting about their male colleagues in the office: six male attorneys who put their income above the results of their cases and the level of care they had for their clients, as if the veracity of the charges in court didn't really matter. What really annoyed Kim was that even though she was also an attorney, the business manager recently revealed that all the male attorneys had a higher salary than she did, though she had been with the firm for six years and was respected for her integrity and success.

Kim had experienced this inequality growing up in South Korea but was surprised to find it in New York, which she expected to be more socially advanced. As Neeya tried to rationalize away the issue, she gave up when she saw Kim's gaze withdraw from eye contact, realizing Kim was also trying to convince herself it wasn't so bad. That would have made it easier to minimize the serious workplace reality.

Back at her desk, Neeya realized that though she enjoyed the time just spent with her friend Kim, it had left her unsettled. In the earlier years of her life, Neeya found it all too easy to avoid thinking about things that made her uncomfortable. Nowadays there was often a brief moment in these situations when she was aware of her real feelings—anger, sadness, or anxiety—but they quickly subsided due to a lack of further attention to them. Neeya was not in denial; she simply acknowledged and then immediately ceased focusing on unpleasant emotions. The uncomfortable ones she ignored and avoided did not really go away. They remained hidden in the veiled compartments of her subconscious, still possessing an energy of their own. Not merely a forgotten memory, these small quanta of psychic effluvia persisted, awaiting the light of understanding gleaned from objective, honest self-reflection—an understanding revealing what lurked within, allowing the energy associated with these feelings to dissipate, as a cloud abandons form in the vast, clear, azure sky.

Neeya often enjoyed spending time in self-reflection, even more so since her extraordinary dream. Although Hank often felt she was too self-absorbed, making comments like, "It is what it is; just ignore it," Neeya was able to lighten her load in this way. During these times of productive inner reflection, Neeya could see how even a thought lasting maybe two seconds—such as, *I hate it when that happens!*—produced a strong emotional response, leaving her with powerful feelings now orphaned from the original fleeting thought. In her moments of clarity, she became aware it was the thought which produced the feeling. To overcome uncomfortable feelings, or even better, to prevent them, she would need to watch her thoughts, trying to keep them neutral, if the effort to keep them positive failed. This was a seriously difficult challenge, as she did not want to live in a fairy-tale world, making believe that nothing bothered her. *No denial for me. I can handle reality, I hope!*

CHAPTER 3

Zune stopped at a scruffy-looking place named Colt's Mart, filled his tank with gas, cleaned his windshield, and walked into the old shop. He quickly noticed the musty smell, stained wooden floor, and a large rack of beef jerky jars on the counter. Two burly, gritty-looking men in worn jeans and rough flannel shirts chatted loudly at a small table, hands glued to their tall bottles of beer. Several empty bottles sat on the floor beside them. Zune would have nodded hello, but they avoided eye contact. There was only plain seltzer, some sodas, and a lot of beer in the coolers. He chose the seltzer.

Approaching the counter to pay, Zune found himself face-to-face with a tall, well-defined woman about thirty with lots of makeup on, wearing snug jeans, a tight red blouse, and dark-leather cowboy boots. Long black hair flowed straight down her back. Her eye contact was very direct as he felt her gaze peering into him. In that fraction of a second, he sensed something familiar.

She was quite attractive and clearly looked like she wouldn't put up with anybody's nonsense. "Yeah?" she voiced, not sounding like it was a question.

Placing the seltzer on the counter, Zune politely informed her, "I also got forty-five dollars of gas."

"That will be seventy-two dollars," she firmly stated. When he asked, she explained tersely, "The pump price is for locals only. Everyone else has a twenty-five-dollar surcharge. Got it?" Zune looked surprised as she scolded, "Don't look at me like that!" He could hear the two guys at the table snickering as they watched the transaction at the counter. Zune paid her the seventy-two dollars.

As Zune turned to leave, an elderly man entered the shop. He sure seemed like a local with his torn, tattered overalls and downcast look. He was mumbling about getting gas on credit since he was out of cash. A tall, large-framed man with the name Colt embroidered on his shirt came over. With a tough tone, he told him, "Cash only, buddy." The old man replied, "Please—" but Colt cut him off, demanding, "Pay in advance, or get out, buddy." As the older man turned to leave, he dropped his car keys. Colt glowered at him, kicking the keys across the floor. The old man just looked at him sheepishly as he slowly stooped over to pick up his keys.

Zune reached in his pocket, pulled out a twenty-dollar bill, and handed it to the old man. With a look of both confusion and gratitude, the man took the bill. Colt was immediately upset by this and roughly challenged Zune. "What the heck do you think you're doing?"

"Just trying to help a guy," Zune responded calmly.

Colt's friend got up too, and both men glared at Zune. "This is my store. Things go my way here," Colt forcefully avowed. "I don't want nobody interfering with nothin', see?" Colt was almost nose-to-nose with Zune as his friend began to inch closer toward Zune. An intimidating look of raw anger bared itself on Colt's face. He would have welcomed a fight. Zune could take care of himself, but there was no reason to let it get physical, especially if it was two against one, and he was certain they would fight dirty.

Zune stayed silent. Colt shoved his shoulder, saying, "It's time you got yourself out of here, mister!" Zune realized it was time to head for the door, which he started to do as he heard Colt's footsteps behind him. Zune was almost at the door when the woman behind the counter implored, "Let him be, Colt, he was just trying to help Clarence."

"Be quiet, Nola!" he ordered. She complied and stood still, her gaze drooping downward.

As Zune turned to look at her, their eyes met. Seeing a flash of the compassion previously hidden behind her edgy manner, he wondered why she would work for, and take orders from, a man like Colt. Wanting to avoid a clearly unsafe confrontation, Zune silently returned the unspoken caring which he sensed in Nola's eyes. There was something left vaguely undone, but this was certainly not the time to explore it.

Zune got in his car, drank some seltzer, and slowly headed further into Bleakville, hoping the rest of the town was not so bad as what he had just experienced. He soon began to realize the name did fit the town, as the houses and stores looked as run-down as the few pedestrians he saw on the sidewalks. Zune started to get a bleak feeling himself in this strange, squalid town. Even so, his desire to better understand why life was so sordid here motivated him to further explore Bleakville and its inhabitants.

Turning off the main drag to see what the backstreets were like, he paused at a corner to finish the seltzer, which went down nicely on this hot, dry, cloudy day. At a shoddy store across from him, three scrubby teens stood in front, yelling at someone inside. One of the teens picked up a rock and threw it through the large plate glass window in front of the store. As they laughed loudly and started running away, an Asian woman followed by an African American man darted outside, yelling at the kids and threatening to call the police. Zune heard the man say, "What's the point? Joey's father is the chief of police, and Joey is just like his father."

Zune realized there were plenty of unkind people here in Bleakville. *I hope these malevolent folks are balanced by others who still have some heart,* he thought to himself.

Zune was getting hungry. When he parked the car and walked into Debby's Diner for some lunch, he was relieved to see things appearing to be normal. A few patrons occupied some of the booths, chatting quietly while eating lunch. Zune chose a seat at the counter, remembering how he once used to enjoy sitting at a bar with friends, telling jokes and watching a ball game on the large screen. He was hoping this meal would be of the same joviality.

After ordering a sandwich and fries, he struck up a conversation with the woman on his left, who was slowly and methodically working her way through a bowl of what looked like stew. She was about sixty or so, with raggedy brown hair, a withered face, and arthritic hands with dirt under the nails. She responded pleasantly enough when Zune said hello, though when he asked, "How are you?" the pleasantry evaporated, her visage darkening as she responded in a dejected tone.

"Eh, same today as yesterday, the same as the day before that, and the same as I'm gonna be tomorrow." A lack of hope was sadly all too evident.

Zune decided to understand her better, asking, "What kind of work do you do here in Bleakville?"—assuming she actually had a job.

"I do house cleaning for some rich folks up on Bounteous Drive."

"How do you like your job?"

"Right, you gotta be kidding me!"

"Oh."

"Who wants to work for mean, spoiled rich people who don't pay squat and treat you like dirt? I think they treat their two dogs better than me."

"Oh, that doesn't sound good. How long have you been working for them?" Zune inquired.

"Way too many years."

"So why don't you find another job?" he cautiously inquired.

The answer came from a middle-aged man seated on the other side of Zune.

"Because there aren't any, and there ain't gonna be any. This is the way it is, and this is the way it's gonna be. Wanda knows just what I mean, don't ya, Wanda?" *It would be very sad if this lack of hope is endemic.*

"I sure do know what you mean, Grady. I wish you were as right about the weather as you are about this. You told me it wasn't gonna rain on Saturday afternoon, and I left my windows open. My living room couch got soaked."

"Uh…" muttered Grady, not defending himself. Zune was sad to see their discontent set in stone.

"And why can't things get better around here?" Zune asked sincerely.

Grady responded again. "Because the rich get richer, and the poor get poorer."

Bleakville's dynamics reminded Zune of an old movie from the 1940s with Humphrey Bogart, *To Have and Have Not*. Although it was more about romance, war, and adventure, the title made Zune wonder how much things really did change. It wasn't only about material things that we have or have not.

"How about you, Grady? Do you have a job?"

"Job? I've been on disability since my back got smashed in a car crash eight years ago. I never was one for a desk job. I'll be sixty-two in a year or so and can start collectin' three hundred seventy-two bucks a month in social security. That'll help. Then I can afford to get my teeth fixed, finally." He flashed an open-mouthed smile at Zune, revealing he only had a few teeth left, and they did not look anywhere near healthy.

Zune got the picture and didn't want to let himself get depressed by hearing more about their bleak lives. He easily changed the topic to the weather and Debby's diner food. She owned the diner, cooked at the griddle, and served the food. Debby gave Zune a look of displeasure when she noticed he left most of the tuna melt sandwich on his plate. She took it personally since it was her grandmother's recipe. Zune found it to be drowning in mayonnaise and maybe starting to go bad. He extended a pleasant goodbye, thanking Grady and Wanda for the conversation. He offered to pay the bill for both of them. Grady, who looked surprised, declined with some irritation, saying, "I may be poor, but I can still pay for my own lunch!" Wanda mumbled, "Thanks," and let Zune pay for her tab.

Soon, Zune was back in his car, continuing to explore more of Bleakville, still hoping for a sign that not all was bleak here. Zune was curious to see what life was like up in the hills of Bounteous Drive. He hoped the contrast between forlorn poverty and affluence would not be overly disturbing, wondering what kept so many people here so far down for so long.

Zune headed north, away from downtown. Just a minute later, he passed a scruffy baseball field with a game in action and could not resist stopping. Zune had played a lot of ball in his youth, and he still loved the game. This was a young women's softball game. Zune pulled his car over to the side of the field near first base so he could watch for a bit.

On the very first play, the batter sliced a line drive deep into left field and took off, running full speed. She slid hard into second base with her front leg up and her spikes high, crashing into the shin of the woman playing shortstop. Zune could hear the sound of the collision, which was as bad as it looked. The woman who got spiked let out a bloodcurdling scream, crashing to the ground in pain. The batter stood up, swaggering on second base with a snarl on her face. Two of the other infielders, outraged, ran over and attacked the batter who had just injured their teammate. Fists were flying, and the fight was on. The players on the field joined in, both dugouts emptied, and a full-scale brawl began as the fans in the bleachers howled.

Wow, this reminds me of the crowds in the Roman Colosseum two thousand years ago! Has anything changed since then? It was bad enough when I stopped watching ice hockey because the refs let the players fight. Am I naive, or are things getting way too violent?

Zune had seen enough. He got back in his car and headed toward the hills. He turned in at the sign for Bounteous Drive, noticing the fully leafed trees, flowering plants, manicured green grass, and freshly paved road. There was an unstaffed entry booth with the gate up, so he continued.

Noticing a lovely looking spot just ahead, Zune parked his car. *Definitely time for a nice stroll here. What a change from town!*

Zune could see sprawling, superbly landscaped large homes at the edge of the park, with a grand flower garden and fountain at its center. He absorbed the fine fragrance of the flowers in the fully blooming garden. An aroma of roses was pervasive. Zune stood still, eyes closed, experiencing only the garden's gift and the splash of the fountain. He felt deeply refreshed in his soul.

"So, do you like my garden?" he was asked by a very direct-sounding woman's voice just behind him. Zune turned to see a well-dressed, attractive woman with dark, green eyes, peering at him in a manner clearly demanding an answer.

"I sure do," Zune responded.

"Good. It's all mine. My plan, my choices of what to grow, and I don't even have to get my hands dirty or my back tired. I have gardeners to do that." She oozed a narcissistic arrogance.

"I used to have a large garden," Zune said softly, recalling all the vegetables he'd planted and harvested, with flowers in every other raised bed. She was interested, yet aloof.

"People in town have no comprehension about what a nice garden actually is. I can't keep a gardener employed for more than one season. They don't appreciate their own work, and they never live up to my expectations. I have to hire two people to do the work of one because they are so slow and lazy. Makes me want to replace the flowers with stone sculptures that don't need any upkeep other than washing off the bird droppings."

They chatted for a while about gardening. She was mentally engaged in the conversation but emotionally cold. *No wonder the gardeners don't stay with her,* Zune surmised.

"I haven't seen you around here before, though I try to only drive through town and not stop in it. I don't like how it looks or feels, and the people are stupid. I'd rather drive the seventy-eight miles to a high-end grocery store in a safe, upscale neighborhood."

"I'm not from here, just passing through," replied Zune.

"Well, you seem like a decent chap, and I need a gardener again. Do you want a job?" Zune would have loved to have a garden like this to tend, but it was inconceivable that he could ever work for this woman. Still, considering how poor the townspeople were, he was curious about the salary, so he asked her.

"I pay $10 an hour. Off the books. No benefits. Working here for me in this lovely environment is benefit enough for the lowlifes from town. And I want things done my way, and only my way, period!"

"Thanks, ma'am, but I'm just passing through on my Journey and can't accept your offer. If I was going to stay around and say yes to you, it would have to be for significantly more than $10 an hour."

She was offended by his refusal of her offer, as people from town are were always looking for a job since there were a lot more of them than there were jobs in Bleakville. "Then I have no use for you." She turned away.

"There is such a difference between what it's like up here on Bounteous Drive and what it's like down in town," Zune thought aloud.

"And why shouldn't it be that way?" she retorted. "I'm smart enough to know how to make a lot of money, just like my parents and their parents before them. Why should I care about the people down below? They are too lazy and too stupid to do anything with their lives, and besides, this is how capitalism works in America." She sounded so proud of her perspective and really didn't need to hear any more from

Zune. He had declined her offer, and she had no further interest in him. Zune realized she would not be open to anything he had to say, so he thanked her for the job offer, complimented her again about the garden, disconnected from her cold glare, and got back in his car.

Seems it's only flowers and trees that prosper in these hills, not its people, Zune concluded as the quiet hum of the car's engine instilled a desire to get back on the open road.

The familiar line from Whitman's poem again came back to him: "Strong and content, I travel the open road." Zune quickly avowed to not let the experience of Bleakville distract him from the contentedness he had been feeling on his Journey along the Infinite Highway of Life.

If how I feel is based on other people's words and attitudes, then I am doomed to be like a robot, automatically reacting to things outside myself. That won't work for me. I will stay steady. Me imperturbe.

At the last corner in town, just before the ramp leading onto the highway, he saw her. It was the woman who worked at Colt's Mart, walking slowly, head down and slumped. She looked rather disheveled. Feeling sympathy, Zune pulled over and greeted her with an upbeat "Hi there!" She looked up at Zune quizzically. It was clear she was in pain, physically as well as emotionally.

"Oh, yeah." Her tone was flat. "You're the guy who tried to help the old man with the keys. Well, hi to you."

Their eyes met, and just like before, he felt a connection he didn't understand. She was very guarded as he tried to engage her in conversation.

"Nola, that's your name, right?" She nodded. "Sorry, but you don't look too well."

"That's nice of you," she uttered with some sarcasm. "But you're right. I feel like crap."

Now that she was standing closer to the car, Zune got out, and they stood face-to-face. As she brushed aside her long black hair, Zune could see a bruise on her wrist and another on one cheek. What caused them was obvious to him.

Zune decided to take a risk. "What happened?" he asked, sounding empathically curious. "Is it that guy Colt, from the gas station?" She did not respond, and he accurately took it for a yes. "I hope you don't live with him, do you?" he wondered aloud. There was another long pause, a tear emerging below the left eye of her once-stern persona. Zune let his caring flow silently to her. He could see she felt it, allowing him enough insight into the depth of her despair.

"Nola, I saw how you cared about that old guy at Colt's Mart. I can see in your face that you are not just the cold, tough woman you outwardly appeared to be. I know there is a whole other side of you."

"And how in God's name does the other side come out in a town like this with a man like that?"

Zune let her incredulous tone and rhetorical question linger in the air before responding. "Can't you make some kind of change in your life, maybe get away from him, away from here, and move somewhere else?"

"No, it's not that simple. I'm stuck here. Probably for good." Although she meant it, Nola was now able to look up and maintain eye contact with Zune. He could tell that on another level, she truly wanted out. Maybe it was only subconsciously, but he sensed her inner struggle to survive in life the way it was, even if she hated it. It was sadly all too simple: she was afraid to leave, afraid of Colt, and fearful of being alone, especially given her lack of resources.

Zune paused, not wanting to act on impulse and upset her. "Nola, I am minutes away from leaving town and getting back on the road. My destination is unclear, yet this Journey to the future calls me, and I must go. Somewhere down the road, there will be another town, one where people are kinder and you won't be smothered the way you are now.

"If you want, Nola, you can ride with me for a while. No strings attached. I promise to absolutely respect you and not bother you in any way. You can get out anytime you want. I can give you some money to help you get settled wherever you land."

The troubling inner conflict was evident in her face. Nola clearly yearned to go with Zune and walk right out of her increasingly miserable life in Bleakville but knew she didn't have the strength or courage to act on it—not now. She was too afraid Colt would come after her, as he had done before.

"I just can't leave. Not now, thanks," she said softly with much gratitude and even a trace of a smile emerging. "Not yet." Nola's smile revealed a glimpse of the real woman within, one with heart, waiting to come alive and blossom. Zune intuitively knew she'd be okay in the long run, though he didn't know how she'd get there or how long it would take her.

"I understand, Nola."

She felt his compassion. "I think you really do. Hey, what's *your* name?"

"Zune."

"Cool name."

"Thanks." They maintained eye contact. She felt his warmth, and it softened her.

"Well, the open road calls me, so I'll get going, Nola."

"Guess so. Have a good Journey, Zune."

"I have a sense we'll meet again, Nola. Maybe some other place sometime."

"Maybe so," she gently responded with a hesitant trace of hopefulness.

"God bless you, Nola."

"Thank you." She knew he truly meant it. *Am I actually feeling his blessing?* "Happy trails, Zune." He gave her a heartful hug and got back in his car.

A moment later, the town was behind him, rapidly fading into the past. Turning onto the Infinite Highway, relinquishing the jarring negativity and hopelessness of Bleakville, the fresh breath of an imminent future beckoned him.

Whitman, again: *healthy, free, the world before me...*

4 CHAPTER

It was almost time for Neeya to leave work when her sister Angela called, inviting her to meet up for drinks and dinner at a favorite lively, upscale place on Seventy-Second Street. "Sure, Angela, that sounds good. I'd like to spend some quality time with my sis!" Neeya was still feeling the uplifting glow of her vivid dream from the other day and was determined to keep it while trying to enjoy Angela's company.

The sign above the entrance proclaimed, "Great Doings Grille." Neeya wondered just what they meant by "doings" as she really didn't want to do anything except relax, eat, and enjoy Angela's company. It was almost six p.m. and still happy hour. Neeya had walked there from her job, wishing she would have worn slacks instead of a skirt ending two inches above her knee with a blouse revealing just a bit of cleavage. With her bright brown eyes, well-defined shape, and pretty face, men were drawn to her. She was apprehensive they would give her the lustful attention which made her uneasy and resentful. Neeya wished men cared more about who she really was and what she thought.

Neeya herself had been wondering just who she really was lately or who she really could be. This produced an uncomfortable state of mind, yet in this moment, she just wanted to let her hair down, have a glass—or maybe two—of a nice white wine and enjoy the company of her sister. This was sometimes hard to do, given Angela's tendency to be callous and uncaring when it suited her. *I hope Angela is in a good mood today and doesn't bring any of her edginess with her.*

Angela flashed a smile accompanied by an enthusiastic greeting as Neeya sat down at the high-top table across from her. Neeya hoped that hanging out with Angela would be a positive experience for both of them that evening. Angela was two years older than Neeya, and though they were quite close when they were young, Neeya was always aware of Angela's competitive nature. She often wondered if it was one of those typical scenarios when a first-born child had to deal with the presence of a new sibling who suddenly got half the love and attention she previously received from their parents. Angela had a crush on a boy named Connor when they were in middle school, but Connor's crush was on Neeya, who still sensed Angela's long-standing resentment.

They enjoyed chatting about old times, though some of their memories of shared events varied widely. Neeya ordered a glass of chardonnay while Angela opted for a daiquiri. They were glad to keep their sisterly connection, especially since both parents had been gone for several years. For the two sisters, a sense of family remained important to them, despite the friction they experienced with each other at times.

Angela was quite attractive and made the most of it. Neeya resembled her mother, who was Latina, while Angela seemed to have inherited more of their Caucasian father's genes, showing none of the classic Latina appearance visible in Neeya's countenance. Neeya's style was basically casual, generic, and middle-class, while Angela was a flashy, modern, urban dresser who liked to show off her physique and be seductive.

"Hey, your beau Hank was able to solve the problem with my Wi-Fi not working last week," Angela told Neeya. "He had to install a new router, but the whole thing only took him an hour."

"Oh, good," Neeya replied, trying to hide her surprise, as Hank had only vaguely mentioned that Angela had called him for tech support. She just couldn't recall that he mentioned actually going over there. "I really liked that cologne he had on," murmured Angela. Neeya responded with a wan half-smile, realizing Angela was trying to make her worried about the visit with Hank. She wanted to trust him, trying to assume it was just Angela being Angela, who had succeeded in making Neeya feel a little uneasy. Neeya decided to ask Hank about this the next time she saw him.

It was getting quite noisy in the Grille now that happy hour was in full swing. The sound system was playing Michael Franti rather loudly. Three TV monitors displayed news and sports. Neeya's attention drifted away as she looked at the screen above and behind Angela, which had on a news station. Angela could see from Neeya's facial expression that it was not good news, and indeed, she was right.

Neeya became increasingly disturbed as she watched scenes of children starving in remote, arid villages of Sudan. The country's infrastructure had collapsed during a severe drought as a civil war raged, and there wasn't nearly enough food, or none at all, for millions of people. The classic images of bony young children with bloated bellies, sad, dark eyes, and tearful parents hovering over them made Neeya feel dismayed.

"Angela, how can I sit here and enjoy drinking wine at $14 a glass and have a big dinner, when people are actually starving to death?" Angela shrugged and replied, "What am I supposed to do about it?"

"Well, sis, you could just care."

"Come on, Neeya, I'm not that coldhearted."

"I hope not," said Neeya earnestly. "Maybe you could make a donation to some organization providing emergency food for people on the verge of starvation."

"Guess so," mumbled Angela.

The headline banner for the next piece of coverage asked, "Is the war between Russia and Ukraine about to resume?" This increased Neeya's uneasiness as she looked at images of destruction from the recent war.

The TV volume was still off as the next news story covered rampant inflation and high unemployment in the US and most of the developed nations. It troubled her to see that the majority of Americans only had enough money in the bank to last two weeks. "Here we are, living like rich people compared to so many of us on the planet. Most people who have enough are oblivious to this stuff. I think I need to do something."

"Go ahead, Neeya."

"I will, Angela."

Neeya perked up as she told Angela of her intention to make a documentary about solutions to a critical humanitarian problem, perhaps somewhere in Africa or Asia, or maybe right here in this massive, modern American city, a video to inspire people to take action and make a difference. Angela was her typically dismissive self, smiling as she said, "I'd be shocked if you could do this, Neeya. I mean, a few home videos are all you've done. You're such an idealist and dreamer, sis. Good luck with that one!"

Neeya resented the thinly veiled sarcastic tone in Angela's voice, letting her know it with a stern glance of reproach. Neeya moved to the seat beside Angela so her eyes could avoid watching the news. The rest of the sisters' time together was spent in mundane chat about their jobs and apartments, polite subjects with little room for disagreement, while they ate the succulent New Orleans salmon special and shared a few laughs.

Neeya tried hard to be kind and forgiving to Angela, but it was often very hard to succeed. Though she enjoyed Angela's company at times, all too often, Neeya felt quite disgruntled, as she did now.

After dinner the two sisters exchanged half-hearted hugs as they departed, heading their own ways. Walking out the door, Neeya almost bumped straight into a man entering the Grille. Their eyes met as they were face-to-face, just inches apart from each other. Both of them uttered a spontaneous "Oh" at the same time, smiling at the synchronicity. He seemed so familiar, though Neeya knew she hadn't met him before. Neither of them said another word. Neeya kept walking, wanting so badly to turn around to see if he was looking at her. She tried hard to fight the urge but at the middle of the sidewalk gave in and looked over her shoulder, seeing him do the same as he went through the doorway.

It was almost unnerving how Neeya felt such a strong vibe, but life was too complicated these days, so she just kept walking straight ahead, toward home, wondering, *What was* that *all about?*

Zune was also surprised to feel her presence so strongly. He had not felt anything like it with a woman in a long time, wondering, *Wow, who was that? Maybe I'll find out some other time. Or maybe not.*

When Neeya was on her way to work, there was rarely a day she didn't stop at Gastro Café for a toasted onion bagel with almond honey cream cheese, washed down with a strong cup of dark-roast coffee. Today was no exception. She successfully made an effort to avoid getting irritated while listening to the conversation between two people in the line ahead of her. *What would be the point of letting them upset me?*

The fifty-ish, casually dressed, middle-class-appearing couple bantered loudly. They bitterly complained how the price of coffee had doubled in the last year and how supply chain issues prevented the café from having any poppy seeds to put on their favorite bagels. At first, Neeya thought it was almost comical. Noticing they had an audience in the line, the couple gladly allowed their resentments to grow louder. They grumbled about the ineptitude of the government and how all the money from their taxes were wasted on building windmills and charging stations for electric vehicles.

A sturdy young man next to them, who Neeya imagined was a construction worker, started to say something about battling global warming. He was angrily dismissed by a nearby young, professionally attired woman, bluntly stating that "Climate change is here, and we just have to live with it. Green energy is not going to prevent three-day storms like the intense Hurricane Stacey last month, leaving many basements in Miami and Baltimore with enough water for wading."

Neeya was surprised and saddened to see how strangers had quicky become so volatile over issues which were once rather abstract but now impacting their experience of daily life. When she heard a comment about the need to replace not just the president but the whole Congress, even if by force, it reminded her all too uncomfortably of January 6th. Neeya knew this was not a productive time to add her two cents to the conversation. She put on her earbuds, tuning into a song by Olivia Rodrigo.

It was summer, so the bagel was still warm when Neeya sat down to eat it at her desk. She was grateful to have her own small office but wished she had a window.

Neeya downed her bagel and was halfway through her coffee when Peter, her boss, came in, asking her to do some research for one of his cases about New York City laws relating to tenancy and leases. Neeya wished Peter could maintain eye contact and not look at her body every time they spoke, though he was otherwise gentlemanly—at least, she thought so. Her quick smile and assurance she would get right on the research belied her real attitude of disinterest. As Neeya took a breath and started her boring, detailed task, the uplifted mood she had clung to since her profound dream the other night continued to fade. It was very challenging to maintain awareness of her inner state while also focusing on her outer life at the same time. Even so, she was able to sustain a vague sense of the dream.

Neeya had played field hockey in high school and softball in college, so when Hank said he had tickets for a baseball game, she was glad to go. It was a rare treat to go to Yankee Stadium on a sunny Saturday afternoon. Neeya hadn't been to a game in seven or eight years. She found herself uncomfortable with the incessant, near-deafening sound bites, horns, commercials, and announcements blasting forth from the huge ballpark speaker system. Neeya thought the game itself should be exciting enough without having to artificially stimulate the fans, many of whom were willing to pay twelve dollars for a barely mediocre, half warm hot dog.

Neeya tried to engage Hank in some meaningful conversation between innings. Since he was way too focused on the activities in the stadium, she decided to hold her thoughts until later. After an exciting end to the game featuring a come-from-behind, home-team rally in the bottom of the ninth inning, they landed back in Manhattan in a small, quiet Mexican restaurant called El Sol.

After Hank finally finished talking about the game, Neeya tried to tell him about her special dream. It was hard to describe something abstract to Hank, especially the mysterious, beneficent people in her dream who reminded her of the Jedi Knights from *Star Wars*. As Neeya expressed her growing concern about the chaos and problems which seemed to be everywhere nowadays in a world increasingly out of control, she could see Hank's attention fading away.

"Oh, they'll take care of it. No nuclear war is coming, and our civilization is not about to collapse," he said rather blandly with an air of self-assurance.

"Maybe not, Hank, but our economy is going down the drain, and it is so upsetting to see millions of hungry refugees in so many countries. Sometimes I worry about a civil war right here in the good ole USA. Also, global warming is way more than a major issue. It has become existential, Hank."

"Come on, Neeya, it's not *that* bad yet."

"It sure is, Hank. Besides, do you think that the politicians and corporations who seem to run the government these days can fix things?"

"Probably not," he murmured.

"Hey, we could use some Jedi Knights who can teach us about the Force and how we can get along with each other," Neeya responded.

"Yeah, right." His half-hearted reply oozed indifference.

"Well, Hank, would you at least agree that this country—or actually, the world—could use some great leaders like Martin Luther King Jr., Gandhi, or Franklin Roosevelt?"

"Sure, but they ain't here, hun, are they?"

"I don't know, but since that dream, I wonder if maybe they're coming," she said hopefully.

"That would be cool, but until then, I will just take care of my daily life and try to have fun." Hank wondered what was going on with her.

Neeya could only nod, as her effort to engage him at a deeper level was clearly failing. The rest of the conversation was about how good the enchilada sauce was and how much he liked having two house-special margaritas. She clearly felt like going her separate way home, declining Hank's offer to stay with him tonight at his apartment. He headed for the door while Neeya sat there recollecting herself as she checked the email on her cell phone.

It was one of those drizzly, cloudy, gray Saturday mornings when time moved slowly. Neeya found herself content to just lounge around, cooking a special breakfast for herself while hoping the new high-res digital video camera she ordered would be delivered today. Some streaming solo piano music gently brightened her mellow mood. *I'm glad I got those really good Bluetooth stereo speakers for the kitchen!*

Neeya later turned on the TV to hear a weather forecaster proclaim, "It's going to be a lousy day, folks, lots of rain." Neeya resented this, thinking, *Who is he to tell me how my day is going to be? Just because it's cloudy and rainy doesn't mean I can't have a good day! How come people are pessimistic so easily?*

Hank had called her a news junkie more than once, and while she denied it, the truth was, she checked the news every couple of hours throughout the day, including right after she woke up and just before bed. Today, Neeya did not want to risk seeing bad news, which could detract from her morning contentedness. Avoiding the news, she took a longer than usual shower, the hot water cascading over her head and down her supple back and legs, warming her deeply throughout.

Neeya cooked an omelet with Swiss cheese and onions inside, accompanied by hash brown potatoes with lots of olives, garlic, and a large piece of buttered, toasted sourdough bread. She reminded herself twice, *It's okay if I just nurture myself a little today. No laundry or paying bills or having to do things other people want me to do.* The taste of her self-determined freedom revealed itself in a serene, sweetened smile. Neeya brushed her hair, quickly evicting the thought that *It would be nice for Hank to be doing the brushing.* Today, she wished to be self-sufficient on all levels.

It was late afternoon when Neeya finally sat down at her computer to check out the news and see the latest developments happening in the world. Neeya's bias was a bit left of center, but she liked to expose herself to all sides of the spectrum. She remained determined to not let any bad news bring her down. That intention did not last long, as she moved between the *New York Times*, ABC, Reddit, CNN, and Fox.

5 CHAPTER

When Neeya arrived at work on Monday morning, Peter, her boss, was standing in front of her office door. "Please come in my office, Neeya." The terse tone of his voice indicated something was amiss. She noticed he didn't give the usual once-over look which had always made her slightly uncomfortable around him.

"Neeya, you've probably heard some rumors in the office that there has been some consideration of merging with another, larger law firm."

"Yes, I have," she replied, "but I really didn't pay any attention."

"Well, we seriously looked into it but decided on a different option." Peter's tone became more serious.

"And what is that option, Peter?" Neeya asked with more than a hint of anxious foreboding in her voice.

"Our financial position has gotten weaker in the last few years, so me and the two other partners in our law firm decided to narrow the focus of our practice to strictly large corporate clients. Our other three attorneys have all chosen to move to Higgins and Burke, the firm where talks almost led to a merger."

Neeya quickly asked, "So what does that mean for me, Peter?"

"That's the hard part, Neeya. You do very good work and people here like you. With half of our attorneys and their paralegals leaving, and the rest of us consolidating our practice, we have significantly less need for support staff. So, since you were the last hired of our parale-gals, unfortunately, we have to let you go. I am so sorry, Neeya."

"Oh" was all Neeya could manage at this point. It wasn't so much that she was disappointed; it was the shock, given her excellent per-formance reviews. Feelings of betrayal arose. She had always given her best, getting very positive feedback from the attorneys.

"What about Kim?" she wondered aloud.

"She will be moving over to Higgins and Burke."

Neeya was stunned to hear this, not due to Kim's choice to change jobs but because they had become close, and it was hurtful to learn Kim had not shared this news with her.

"So, Peter, when is this change taking place?"

"The three attorneys who are leaving will do so as soon as they wrap up their current cases, which will take about a month." Peter avoided eye contact with Neeya while scrounging for the right words. Then they emerged bluntly.

"Neeya, we have decided to terminate your employment immediately."

"What?" She was incredulous.

Peter was even more terse now. "It has become common practice these days to let someone go immediately after informing them their employment is being terminated. It helps avoid things from getting uncomfortable for everyone, or worse."

"Are you telling me that immediately means today, Peter?"

"Yes, Neeya, not only today, but it means now." Neeya just stood there, trying to keep a lid on the anger arising within her. She literally bit her tongue in an effort not to vehemently curse him out.

"Because you have been such a valued employee, we are giving you four months of severance pay."

Her "Gee, thanks" was bitterly sarcastic.

"There are some cardboard boxes in the utility closet if you need them for your belongings. Can you please give me your keys, Neeya?"

Neeya tossed her keys to him, though it was more like she threw them at him, making a loud clang as they hit the coffee mug in his hand. *I hope it cracked.* She got up abruptly, leaving the office without another word, feeling pleased knowing she would never have to look him in the face or talk to him again.

Packing up her belongings, anger morphed into feeling she was discarded because she was useless. There was no answer when Neeya knocked on Kim's office door, so she called Kim on her cell phone. Neeya challenged Kim about why she didn't tell her of the coming changes at work. Kim was profusely apologetic, sounding like she was about to cry as she described having to sign a nondisclosure agreement preventing her from discussing the merger or other changes. Neeya felt like they were close enough for Kim to have trusted her enough to at least give a hint of what was about to transpire.

The bastards! It sure is easier to find a job while you are still employed. At least I can collect unemployment.

Neeya kept a streamlined office and was able to fit all her personal items into one large box. She left her two potted plants there, not wanting to take home any negative reminders she might later associate with the trauma of being fired. She cleared out her desk drawers and within ten minutes was packed and ready to go. Neeya left as quickly as she could, not wanting to say goodbye to anyone. They all seemed to be adversaries now anyway.

Neeya flagged down a taxi and soon arrived home, where she plopped down on her couch, trying to process what had just happened. This was, sadly, too easy to do. *It was a typical corporate scenario,* she thought. *Big changes affecting little people. I was just one of those dispensable little people.*

It didn't take long before Neeya's shock, resentment, and disappointment peaked. It felt terrible. However, it slowly began to ebb a bit as she realized the future was not written yet. It was waiting for her to create it. This realization emanated from a place of clarity within, somewhere behind all those harshly negative thoughts and feelings accompanied by the typical wonderings of "Why me?" and "What next?" They were momentarily replaced by a feeling of freedom. This led Neeya to recall her aspiration to make documentaries. It was her conscience calling, and she heard it. Neeya decided right then to banish her negative reactions, feeling like they would give away her power to the forces causing her distress. Neeya was highly motivated not to let external factors determine how she felt or to disturb her sense of self. Well, it didn't last very long. A moment later she felt sad, angry and anxious all at once.

Neeya sought some external comfort. She called Hank and told him what had happened, and he agreed to leave work early to come over and be with her.

When Hank arrived, Neeya vented about losing her job, sharing all the traumatic thoughts and feelings coursing through her psyche. Hank did his best to be supportive, but Neeya felt it was more like pity than sympathy. She did not like being pitied since it didn't really help. When he kept repeating, "I feel so sorry for you, Neeya," she kept thinking, *Gee, that's about what he feels, it's not really about what I feel. He could've just acknowledged what I'm feeling and what it's like to get fired unexpectedly. He could have said something like what a good paralegal I am and how I work so hard, or how upset I seem. Yeah, but he just lacks the insight on how to give me the emotional support I truly need.*

Neeya became quiet and just sat there gazing out the window at the little bit of gray sky visible from her urban apartment. Hank began to caress her arm, but Neeya pulled back. She began to think about how her sister Angela had mentioned Hank had spent time at her place, troubleshooting the Wi-Fi. The way Angela related the story made Neeya wonder if something had actually happened between her sister and Hank. Angela had subtly yet deftly inferred the possibility. Neeya knew it was something Angela was certainly capable of doing, even enjoying it as a twisted victory over her. Neeya had avoided asking Hank, but in this moment when life had suddenly become upended by an unexpected loss of her job, she knew she could not tolerate any more uncertainty. Neeya decided to ask Hank, now, straight out.

"What are you thinking, Neeya? You suddenly have that faraway look in your eyes." She didn't need to pause and consider her response to him.

"Well, Hank, I was remembering how Angela told me you went to her apartment recently to help out with her Wi-Fi connectivity. I thought it was kinda weird that you never mentioned it to me."

"Oh, I didn't mention that? Sorry." Neeya felt like Hank was trying a little too hard to sound sincere.

"No, you didn't, Hank. What did you do there?"

"I installed a new 5G router for her. The old one wasn't working anymore."

"Did you stay awhile and hang out with her?"

Hank began to feel uneasy, not knowing what Angela might have told her and hoping to avoid getting caught in a lie. Neeya noticed.

"Yes, I did, for a little while."

"Did she offer you a drink?" Neeya observed Hank starting to squirm a bit. She was already hearing and seeing enough to use her womanly intuition to realize something had gone on between them.

"Yeah," replied Hank uneasily. He was blushing a deep pink now.

"So, what did you have to drink, Hank?"

"We each had two gin and tonics."

"The way my sister makes them really strong, I'm guessing it was actually like having four gin and tonics. You probably were really feeling it."

"Yeah." Hank's face was getting red now.

"Is that when she got seductive with you?"

"C'mon, Neeya!" Hank was protesting and pleading at the same time.

"What was she wearing, Hank?" The question further evoked his fear of saying something which contradicted what Angela may have already said to Neeya. He was getting an ugly feeling of being defeated, and he didn't like it.

"Okay…I'll tell you. She had on a short, snug black skirt with a purple tank top cut kinda low. Oh, and she was barefoot."

Neeya was not surprised. Now she had to hear Hank tell the truth. "And did you get the hots for her, Hank?" His throat tightened up, and he could only manage a shrug at this point.

"So, Angela was coming on to you big-time, wasn't she?"

"Kind of, yeah."

"Then what?"

Hank was rapidly losing the ability to defend himself as Neeya got closer to the truth. His voice softened squeamishly.

"Okay, Neeya, you really want to know?" He was feeling guilty, tears emerging, fearing Neeya's reaction.

"You know I do, Hank. Maybe you can convince me otherwise, but I don't want to live with a hidden lie. I have too much integrity for that!"

"She stood behind me and started massaging my neck and shoulders, thanking me for helping with her router. Then she started saying things, provocative things, and telling me how attractive I am. She started pressing against me as her hands were caressing me. I wanted to say stop and pull away from her, but she was so seductive, and I guess I was feeling the alcohol."

"So, you slept with her, didn't you, Hank?" Neeya's tone was challenging and accusatory. For her, the alcohol was absolutely no excuse. The disgust in her voice unnerved Hank, who again could only nod sheepishly.

"I felt so terrible afterward. I felt really guilty for cheating on you. I made her promise not to tell. It will never happen again, Neeya, never. Really, Neeya, never, ever, with anyone!"

Neeya was silent. It was another major betrayal. *Twice in one day!* She didn't want to let Hank see it, but she was devastated. It was already too far gone for her to even begin to hear his apology. He had crossed a red line, big-time, one that should never be crossed. They had agreed to be monogamous, so the cheating itself was too much for her to recover from, but with her sister…! *I feel so humiliated. What a jerk he is!*

Neeya was done with him completely, just like that. Hank could tell by the look in her eyes. When he started to continue apologizing, she cut him short, angrily ordering him to shut up.

"We're *done*, Hank! You betrayed me. I can never forgive you, and I can never trust you again."

"C'mon, Neeya, let's talk. We can work through this. I love you."

"Maybe you didn't hear me, Hank. It's over! I want you to leave, now!"

Hank saw all too painfully that she totally meant it. He had lost her for good. Neeya didn't care that he was crying. In fact, she didn't want to look at him.

"I'm so, so sorry, Neeya," he mumbled, slowly shuffling toward the door, head bowed down. Hank turned toward her, but before he spoke, she gave his back a firm push right out the door. Neeya slammed the door behind him, trying to keep a grip on the rage inside her.

She leaned over the couch, sinking down onto it with a thud. Seething with anger at Hank for cheating with her sister, Neeya affirmed to herself that she hated Angela for seducing him. It was Angela's sick way of competing with Neeya, acting out some distorted need to avenge the many imaginary wounds Neeya had caused her when they were growing up. Neeya knew Angela had some significant issues, but this was no excuse. "I'm done with her too!" she said aloud. Neeya reached for the phone to call Angela and tell her off but decided Angela might enjoy hearing her vent. Neeya didn't want to give her the satisfaction, and slammed down the phone. *I'd rather be done with her. She won't be hearing from me anytime soon, or maybe anytime at all!*

Hank was gone. Her job was gone. Neeya buried her face into the couch, crying with the pain of two major losses and betrayals within hours. She was overwhelmed and dismayed. The couch cushion grew damp with her tears.

Neeya lay there, unable to let go of it all, her rapid, uncontrolled thoughts violently swirling. After an hour she finally calmed herself emotionally, allowing thoughts to slow down enough so that she had some semblance of control over her mind. The effort to manage her state of mind resulted in a long, loud sigh, as an intense shudder rippled through her body, releasing toxic tension. Then an inner peacefulness, her long-lost friend, found its way home after lying dormant for way too long. Soon, she fell asleep.

CHAPTER 6

As Neeya began to become conscious the next morning after a rest-less night with little sleep, it dawned on her: *I'm not going to work today*. She was jobless and unwanted. Laid off would be a nicer way of putting it, since she felt like she was fired outright. Despite her efforts to frame it in a positive light with thoughts about creating her own future, Neeya felt rejected and dejected. Then, as her mind awakened more clearly, the impact of Hank's betrayal joined forces with the trauma of losing her job. Her eyes felt heavy as they slowly closed again, leaving her feeling adrift at sea on a raft, alone. *I am so bummed, to the max. I just don't have any reason to get out of bed and do anything.* Her state of mind lasted too many dreary hours.

In an attempt to free herself from sinking further into a deeply depressed state, Neeya got up, heading for the coffee pot in her kitchen, thankful in advance for the boost caffeine might provide. *This makes me feel like an addict, hoping a drug will wake me up and boost my mood.* With a hot brew of dark roast in her favorite ceramic mug, Neeya sat down in front of the TV, hoping that watching news about the rest of the world might keep her away from her own morose feelings.

The first story covered was about massive civil unrest in Venezuela and Lebanon. Their economies had collapsed, with severe shortages of food and many other goods. The electric grids were only working for a couple of hours a day. Scenes of major protests in the streets were alarming to Neeya. *I can't believe how so many people are hurting so badly. Oh no! Did that many people really kill themselves last week?*

It wasn't any better in the eurozone, with inflation running over eighteen percent and unemployment at record highs. The governments of Great Britain, Denmark, and Italy recently had no-confidence votes. People were out in the streets by the millions in Greece and Germany, demanding their governments do something yet knowing they were unable to remedy the out-of-control degradation of their economies. Intensely polarized bipartisanship caused governments to be unable to make any productive decisions. The political focus deteriorated into combative conflict rather than any semblance of bipartisanship resulting in decisions helpful to the populace. Citizens' way of life was incredibly disrupted, with great fear it would never return to what "normal" used to be. Protests and counterprotests often led to violence. *Why can't we just figure out how to get along with each other?* Neeya knew that if people were unable to let go of differences enough to compromise and cooperate with each other, things would get worse, not better. *I definitely do not want to imagine what that would be like!*

Neeya was awed to watch a video clip of an ice shelf the size of Ohio slowly crumbling off of Greenland and into the ocean, learning it would cause sea levels to rise almost a foot in the coming year. *The ice age is long gone, but here comes the wet age!*

Scenes of brutal civil war in Central Africa made her nauseous, and at that point, the TV had to go off. Her super-high-def smart TV was not working right all the time, and though she had ordered a new one online seven weeks ago, a text message from the manufacturer stated,

"Due to ongoing supply chain disruptions, no delivery date update is currently available." *Oh, crap.*

Years ago, Neeya had occasionally tuned into the Good News Station but was disappointed she couldn't find it today and assumed it was long gone. Neeya knew there were plenty of people and organizations trying to do good things and be helpful toward each other but thought, *It just doesn't seem like enough right now! I am so worried about what's happening to our planet!* She did find thegoodnewsnetwork.org but figured stories about an eighty-four-year-old man who sailed around the world by himself, traffic ticket quotas for police being banned, or food companies cutting harmful additives were simply not enough to deal with the profound problems now facing the world. She was seriously troubled. *Well, if we created all these major problems, then we should be able to solve them.* She was less than successful at convincing herself of this happening in the foreseeable future.

I've had it with all this bad news. I have enough bad news of my own lately. Bed, here I come... Neeya spent the rest of the day in bed, getting up only for the bathroom a few times, eating nothing, and drinking just apple juice and water. An occasional thought of what she might do with her life entered her mind but lasted only seconds, as she just could not summon up the energy to imagine something good. She wallowed in self-pity and could not escape it.

The worst part of all this for Neeya were troubling thoughts of hopelessness, leaving her wondering, *Where are the leaders who can help us solve our crises? How can God let this happen in the world?* At this point she was not really sure what she believed about God, yet her plea spontaneously emerged anyway.

Neeya spent the next three days alone in her apartment. When Kim eventually called to check in on her, Neeya was very grateful to feel Kim's compassion and deep concern for her welfare. It felt so different than Hank's verbalization of pity. Kim was just about the only person in Neeya's life who really cared for her on a deep level, the level where true friendship and love lived. Kim was good medicine for Neeya's heart. After the phone call with Kim, Neeya felt like she was beginning to emerge from the dark lair of despair she'd let envelop her. *I love you, Kim!*

Later that afternoon, gazing out the window at a blue sky with white wisps of clouds gliding eastward in slow motion, Neeya felt the impulse to go outside and refresh her soul. *I've had it with this depressed crap. I gotta get out in the sun and fresh air and begin to live again.*

Well, it was easier said than done. Neeya slowly walked along the loud, crowded city streets as sirens wailed, horns honked, truck engines echoed, and hip-hop music blared. The stimulation to her senses was way too much. Her attention turned back inward again. It was a form of self-protection from an external world of abrasive intensity and the furtive glances of passersby. It was just too much for her, too soon.

Back home in the safe, quiet sanctuary her apartment granted, the anger, self-pity, and boggling betrayal slowly abated. Neeya was left feeling numb and empty. Recent news coverage of strife and hunger around the world arose in her mind, making it hard to imagine it would all work out okay sometime for her and for everyone else as well.

Even if I do craft a great documentary, how many people will actually see it? Will it really make a difference? How can I—or anyone—do some-

thing to keep humanity from going off the deep end? It was a rhetorical question she was not about to answer. Neeya yearned to forget forlorn feelings and the haunting, hopeless questions taking turns having their way with her mind. Briefly recalling her profound dream provided some solace. Eventually, she drifted off to sleep.

Having fallen deeply asleep at dusk, it was a long time until tomorrow dawned on the horizon. Neeya was briefly pleased to be awakened by the song of a bird chirping loudly outside her open window—a welcomed change from the unruly noise of the city streets which greeted her daily arising. Even so, her mood was flat and numb, yet at least not so negative as it had been these last few days. By lunchtime, as her appetite called out for the first time in days, a desire arose for some Indian food she could take out from Mt. Kailash, a nearby Indian restaurant she loved to frequent. Neeya showered, got dressed in an old pair of jeans and a gray sweatshirt, and headed out the door into the city streets for some samosa and tandoori chicken. In the restaurant, the exotic aromas, surreal music, and mystical paintings on the wall almost transported her to India. The warm bag of food in her hands was soothing, and for the first time in four days, Neeya was hungry. "Oh my; I'm salivating," she uttered aloud, hoping no one heard her.

On the way back home, just three blocks from her apartment, Neeya noticed a simple, small storefront called Common Community. It had some posters in the window regarding upcoming events. She was intrigued by the name of a place she had never noticed before, deciding to venture inside rather cautiously. She did not want to find herself being snagged by a zealous staff member who was looking for volunteers or donations.

Neeya was mildly interested in event postings about enhancing community resilience and another one on conflict resolution yet was still too numb inside to really care or want to attend anything. The Indian food waited to be eaten, and Neeya was motivated to accommodate. As she turned to leave, she noticed a flyer in bold blue-and-yellow colors for a talk titled, "Goodwill Is the Answer." She read it, noticing the time and date of the event, and then left. The flyer intrigued her, but this faded as she arrived back home and began to eat. Neeya was not even halfway through her zesty dinner when she suddenly felt full. A leftover vestige of her recent despair, numbness returned, and the couch beckoned. In a moment she was horizontal, hoping to survive the wave of depression seeking to wash through her. Sleep protected her from the worst as dreams found their way elsewhere.

When Neeya awoke a couple of hours later, her first thought was of the flyer she saw for the talk about goodwill. In a sudden moment of clarity, she decided to attend the event. Neeya wasn't sure why, but the decision to go was made, and there was no need to think about it further. The talk was tomorrow evening, and that felt many miles away. Right now, sadness ruled.

Neeya arose to another day of grayness. At least, this was how she felt, despite the mix of sun and clouds. Meandering around her apartment, Neeya picked up a novel she was reading, putting it down each time after five or so pages, unable to stay focused.

Neeya again felt the need for some support and human contact, so she called Kim, hoping she'd be home to take the call since it was a Saturday. Neeya was disappointed to hear the call go straight to voicemail and left Kim a message anyway. "Hey, Kim, it's me, Neeya. Hope you're doing good. Guess I'm not. I'm trying to deny that I'm depressed. Just feeling blah cause of, you know, Hank and my job. Maybe I should say because of my ex and my old job, since I don't have either anymore. I really have no idea what I want to do with my life right now. Definitely no more of that paralegal stuff, and I have no idea how to get into the world of making documentaries. Just trying to get myself through the day. Oh well, enough for now. Talk later. Love ya."

It somehow helped to have verbalized aloud to Kim, even though it was a one-sided conversation. Neeya took a long, hot shower, letting the water avail the top of her head, soothing her brain and soul. She imagined it was washing away all the bad vibes of the last few days. Maybe it was. Drying off, Neeya recalled how Hank had often praised her good looks, but she immediately let go of the thought, as she felt the all-too-familiar disgust trying to rear its ugly head. She already had enough of that. She was clean now, and it felt good.

Current-events junkie that she was, Neeya checked out the news on a few of her favorite streaming stations. She was stunned to see the intensive inferno of massive wildfires in California and Australia. There was some coverage about this the other day, and it was hard to imagine that these flaming monsters could now be stopped, even if a few thousand firefighters were working at it. The next scene was the opposite.

In China, four days of nonstop, torrential rainstorms had flooded the Yellow River, causing a major dam to break. Many towns downstream were flooded. She wondered if she heard it accurately—that two million people had their homes washed away and more than three hundred farms were obliterated in just one day. *And this is only the beginning of climate change?* Neeya was too distraught to let herself imagine what was happening right this moment to all those people. She could not let her mind go there. She felt helpless to do anything about it. *I could donate a hundred dollars to the Red Cross or the UN Refugee Program, but would that really help? Not much, but I gotta do something! What that is, I don't really know, and I sure can't solve it today, considering how lousy I feel.* The excuse gave her a sense of relief.

Before Neeya could turn off the news, her attention was captured by a clip about chaotic street protests in multiple US cities over the terrible state of the economy and its impact on people's everyday lives—out-of-control inflation, super high unemployment, plus never-ending supply chain issues causing a lack of so many items always taken for granted. These problems were bad enough, but what really troubled Neeya were the violent fights breaking out between protesters and counter-protesters. *It is so weird*, she reflected. They agreed on the severity of the problems but were worlds apart on the causes and solutions. She was surprised to see that most people rioting looked like everyday folks from all walks of life. No extreme-right-wing paramilitary groups, and no radical leftists. Just regular people. *Oh crap! It looks like a civil war out there! I wish people could just disagree better.* Off went the news.

Now, Neeya was struggling to not allow herself to get overly distressed by the disturbing images she had just ingested. It was a long afternoon, but by early evening, Neeya drummed up enough internal resources to get herself moving. She headed out for the talk at Common Community, though she was not hoping for much.

The unassuming appearance of the storefront made it easier for Neeya to enter the building. Neeya purposely arrived just moments before the scheduled start of the program. She would have liked to be invisible, but since it was not really possible, Neeya determined to remain as low profile as possible. The last thing she wanted to do was get caught up in conversations with strangers who had either too much to say or wanted to know what she was thinking. *I just want to listen tonight and not talk to anybody, okay?*

Neeya wore loose-fitting, dark-green cargo pants and an extra-large, gray, long-sleeved T-shirt. It never occurred to her to wear makeup, like the little bit she would put on when she went to work. Her hair was pulled back in a tight ponytail, her brown, well-worn sneakers feeling comfy underfoot. Neeya didn't want to be noticed. In the lobby, her eyes rested upon a poster: "Goodwill Is Love in Action." In the center was an illustration of a man who she imagined was supposed to be saintly. The deep simplicity of the message rang true for her, though she shied away from any religious nuance.

Neeya slowly entered the room where the talk was to be held, finding most of the forty or so wooden seats already filled. She scanned the room and briefly made eye contact with a man standing nearby. *Do I know him?* Neeya immediately felt a strong sense of recognition but couldn't place it. *Wow! Who is he? I better sit down before I find out.*

Zune felt the same vibe. He remembered her face and the brief moment when they'd passed each other in the doorway of the Great Doings Grille a couple of weeks ago. He intuitively knew this was one of those meant-to-be crossings of paths. In the same moment, he was aware there was no need to act on it now, especially as he could see Neeya's reaction was both recognition and withdrawal. Zune had taught himself to be patient, which was incredibly hard work, and it paid off in the long run. Over the years he had learned to trust his intuition. The real challenge was keeping clear and calm enough in the midst of daily life to be able to hear his conscience and then follow it. He sat down in a row behind Neeya, a few seats to the side of her. *Can't let myself get distracted too easily. Gotta keep this detour from the Infinite Highway short.* Despite his effort to control his attention, Zune wondered, *Why does she remind me of Nola from Bleakville?*

As the speaker was being introduced, Neeya risked a quick scan of the room, again wondering, *Who is that guy?* She found him just a few feet away. He was looking at the speaker, allowing Neeya time to admire a profile revealing both sensitivity and strength. He was handsome, for sure. When she tried to gain more of a sense of who he was, the speaker's introduction was over, and it was time for Neeya to look up front and listen. She looked away from him as the talk began, yet still felt intrigued.

Neeya was concerned that since the place had a bit of a New Age feel, the speaker might be a man dressed all in white, trying to mimic a Hindu guru. She was glad to see a well-dressed, very-short-haired, middle-aged African American woman at the podium. Grace Summers was tall, slim, and stately. Her speech was clear and lucid. She evinced a refined, almost elegant way about her, yet had a kind of down-home, warm style, as if you were sitting in her living room listening to her speak directly to you.

"It's probably safe to assume many of you folks are here because you are aware our world is in a rather troubled state today. Hopefully, you

are considering what you may be able to do about it. I am so grateful for that! Most people, even the ones who care, feel overwhelmed,
believing they are powerless—that the little part they can play is just
a drop in the ocean and won't really make a difference. That's understandable. But consider that the ocean is made up of billions and tril-
lions of drops, and if each one of us did our little part, all together, it
can, and will, make a difference."

Neeya liked the sincerity and sound of Grace's voice. This allowed
her to become open and receptive to what Grace was saying. After
taking just a moment to remind the audience about the conflict, polarization, mistrust, and misinformation which had become all too pervasive in this century, Grace began to explain how the spread of goodwill, on a wide scale, can make all the difference.

It came to Neeya's mind that on Christmas Day, there is that line
about peace on earth and goodwill to all. She thought about how
people embrace it and are warm and kind to each other on that day.
*I wonder why we have the Christmas spirit only one day a year? Then we
go back to our normal lives, and the door of our heart is not so open anymore. Gee whiz.* She decided to ponder on that one later.

Grace continued. "Goodwill is actually an energy which flows
through us, which we can express in our words and actions. It's been
said that energy follows thought. If this is true, our positive thoughts
do go out into the field of human consciousness and can play a role
in nurturing one another. This is why we are responsible not just for
what we do, but also for what we think and feel. It's all energy."

Grace suggested, "When we see ourselves as part of the life of the
one humanity, we find ourselves inspired to consider what is good for
all. We can do so by embracing and using the energy of goodwill in

our work for the common good. Let's consider that what we have in common includes the mineral, vegetable, and animal kingdoms, as well as the human kingdom and whatever may lie beyond.

"Perhaps the most practical way to care for the common good is to embrace the principle of sharing. Sounds like a daydream, but it really can be that simple. I am not talking about socialism. Sharing is an expression of goodwill.

"Community is also what we have in common, even if we live alone. Through cooperation to meet the needs of our communities, we are working with goodwill. How we do so is up to each of us, in our own way.

"Here is my whole talk in one sentence: Goodwill can transform our world! This can happen through simple acts of kindness anywhere, everywhere."

Neeya glanced at that interesting man again, noticing how deeply attentive he was to Grace, his eyes staying focused on her. Neeya remained intrigued, feeling drawn to him, though she did not want to miss a word Grace was saying.

"Maybe you have heard the greeting often used in India—'Namaste.' It means, 'I honor the light within you.' This is what happens when we truly regard another human being, especially when it comes from the heart. What that light is, well, that's another lecture some other time," Grace said, smiling broadly. "I hope you find ways to inspire others to spread goodwill. The world desperately depends on it, especially now. Please consider reflecting on goodwill and see what you can do with it."

By this point, Neeya felt inspired. As the talk was finishing up, forgotten were Hank's betrayal and the loss of her job. Grace's words had rekindled an altruism she had almost forgotten. Now she was feeling it again. Neeya wanted to hold onto it, and she knew she would. *Maybe that's my prescription to get out of the funk I've been lost in.*

When Grace finished her talk, the upbeat mood in the room was palpable. As John Lennon's song "Imagine" came on over the speakers, Neeya found herself humming along. She stood up and released a long, slow, audible sigh. Turning to look for that intriguing man again, there he was, just a couple of feet away, approaching her. His beautiful blue eyes were looking directly into hers as they encountered each other without speaking.

"Hi," he said in a most pleasant-sounding voice. It took a moment before Neeya could collect herself and say "Hi" back to him. *He seems so very familiar...but we've never met before, right?*

"Do you remember me?" he asked her. She paused before being able to acknowledge him with, "Well, I seem to recognize you, but I can't say I remember you." After another silent pause, it came back to her. *Oh yeah, the guy I saw coming out of the Grille the night I had dinner with Angela. Wow!*

"We passed by each other in the doorway of that restaurant a couple of weeks ago, true?" Neeya asked. His magnetic, silent smile let her know she was right.

Simultaneously, they both said, "I wondered if—" stopping abruptly as they voiced the same thought at the same time. Their shared laugh was a perfect icebreaker. In an unrehearsed delivery, Neeya and Zune finished the sentence together: "—I was going to see you again."

It felt so lovely for Neeya to be in Zune's presence, despite a passing thought that *I'm not getting involved with him on some rebound kind of thing because I just fired Hank.* Intending to resume his travels on the Infinite Highway soon, Zune was not interested in romance these days, so there was really no need for Neeya to worry. He was not eyeing her like some hungry guy on the street or in a bar. She was immediately comfortable interacting with him. Actually, she was more than comfortable.

As they began to chat about Grace's talk, Neeya and Zune quickly felt a special vibe developing between them. He really liked her suggestion that what the world needed was simply the Christmas spirit 365 days a year, not just on one day.

"Maybe we can figure out how to make that happen," Neeya offered cautiously.

"Maybe so, but the state of things is so bad, I think we may need to find some kind of Messiah type dude to help out," said Zune.

"Yeah, unless it turns out to be a woman," she replied.

"Guess it doesn't matter, uh…." He wanted to say her name and realized he didn't know it yet. She noticed.

"Hey you, my name is Neeya."

"Nice name." He meant it. "My name is Zune."

Neeya reached out, offering her hand to shake. She wanted to give him a hug but felt it was too much, too soon. He took her hand in both of his. It felt so very nice. Neeya liked the warmth of the physical touch, but what really got her was the feeling they were deeply simpatico. She wondered if it was a spiritual connection, though she wasn't exactly sure what that meant.

Zune found it exceptionally easy to talk with Neeya as the conversation flowed fluidly. Other than his short stay in Bleakville, where he'd interacted with Nola and the arrogant woman who'd wanted to hire him as a gardener, Zune hadn't had any meaningful contact with a woman in a long time. Being in Neeya's presence felt good. Even so, the unyielding determination to maintain his Journey on the path into the future never wavered, nor did his intention not to get distracted. However, it felt right to continue what he originally thought was going to be only a very short detour in this big city. Getting to know Neeya seemed like a meaningful part of this detour, however long it may be.

Despite how nice it felt to be with Zune, Neeya began to feel depleted, experiencing a need to withdraw and go back to her apartment. There, she could be alone with no challenges other than keeping her mood from slipping down the steep slope of self-pity back into depression. *This is really, really cool, but I need to get back home,* she almost said aloud.

They agreed to meet again. Neeya was so pleased Zune offered his cell phone number but didn't ask for hers. She was glad that in their hug goodbye, he only gently grasped her upper arms without pressing himself against her at all. His cheek grazed hers, and Neeya felt the touch viscerally. Neeya was surprised how a friendly, platonic hug could feel so exquisite. Zune was not wearing cologne, and the aroma of his physicality made her want to maintain the hug, but he pulled back, leaving her with his essence lingering. She was exceedingly intrigued.

Zune knew something special awaited but figured it was best not to think about it now and just let life unfold. *I don't have to know the future today. It can reveal itself tomorrow.* He wasn't sure if there really was anything destined here. His conscience reminded him that his soul's path was creating itself via his Journey on the Infinite Highway of Life. *Feels absolutely fine to be traveling some of that road with Neeya, if it is meant to be. Inshallah.*

7 CHAPTER

S afe and snug back in her apartment, the glow from the talk on goodwill and the experience of meeting Zune slowly faded as sleep embraced Neeya. Awakening the next morning without Zune or Grace around, she found herself feeling lonely. It was a good sign, though, that Neeya didn't even think about Hank. The contrast between the upbeat inspiration of last night and the damp, gray, cloudy morning produced a sense of emptiness.

All that stuff last night was great. Themes of goodwill, sharing, meeting that guy Zune…but what am I supposed to do about it? About anything? What can I actually do with my petty little life? Yeah, there's my daydream of making a documentary, but, uhhhhh.

The rabbit hole of an unexpectedly resumed depression was dark and deep now. Its tug felt strong. A line of least resistance called her, searching for the opening a lack of hope, or a surrender to helplessness may have provided. *Someone keep me from going there, please!* It was more of a demand than a prayer.

As Neeya wondered how in this world she could find some peace today, recollections of rare moments from her childhood came back to her, moments when she was in church and it felt good to be there. Those times were long gone, and her faith was not too far behind nowadays. Even so, it occurred to Neeya to go to a church.

Neeya wasn't even sure what she believed about God and life now. She wasn't atheistic; she just didn't have a worldview or spiritual perspective which could explain what it was all about in an acceptable way. Unanswered were the eternal questions regarding the meaning of life and how it all worked. She was curious though. Her desire to go to church was a yearning to fathom a deeper meaning to life than the everyday, mundane occurrences which ensnare us in dimensions of troubled emotion, inner turmoil, and waves of discontent. Neeya just wanted to find some peace, something to soothe her troubled soul—maybe some clarity about what to do next with her life. So, Neeya got herself together and walked to the massive gothic cathedral uptown.

An atmosphere of deep reverence permeated this cathedral. Even those with no particular religious interest could feel it, however undefinable it may have been. For the devoted, it is a place where heaven reaches down to touch earth, and where earth stretches up to meet heaven. For Neeya, it offered a safe, peaceful atmosphere. A feeling of things sacred awoke within her. *This is where I feel the sacred. I know there is something holy here, whatever holy actually is. And what does peace truly feel like?*

On this early Tuesday morning, Neeya found herself alone in a small chapel just off the main hall. Sitting down in an empty pew, her eyes closed as she made an effort to let go of the stress and pain of the last few weeks—to release essentially everything but this moment. But one has to admit feeling it in order to be able to let go of it. Otherwise, we repress, internalize, and make believe it's not still there.

Neeya was so grateful to have the cozy little chapel all to herself. Tears welled up, easing down her cheeks, silently carrying away the detritus of her psyche and all the emotions which felt so bad lately, emotions which now had no use. She saw them as a distraction from moving forward with life, an unnecessary anchor welding her to limitless quagmires of drama in a chaotic world rapidly losing most of its meaning. She knew it, not resisting, allowing herself a cathartic cry.

Neeya hoped she would not be left empty and bereft with this release of her woes as she made an effort to be open for whatever may be coming. Remembering her vivid dream of the benevolent ones in the blue room, she imagined the arrival of those special ones—*Or whoever is actually coming.* Ever so vaguely, she became aware of the dream as a link to a gently beckoning future.

It's so strange to come here. I gave up trying to find meaning in church buildings long ago. It's so hard to relate to the ancient biblical stuff now, in the twenty-first century. It just doesn't do it for me anymore, even though I liked it as a child. Yet here I am seeking solace in a church. Huh!

Neeya's heart slowly began to feel soothed and serene. Her mind became calm.

She recalled her altruistic yearnings yet had no idea what to do with them other than recent vague daydreams of videography. She was not ready to think concretely. Neeya just wanted to feel the peace of the moment.

Neeya became aware of soft footsteps and a presence nearby. She looked over to see an older, distinguished-looking man, tall and slender with a shock of white hair, his kind face looking at her with deep concern and sympathy. Gesturing to ask if he could come closer, he softly asked, "Okay?" Neeya felt no apprehension, thankfully accepting his offer. She intuitively trusted the situation. He smiled warmly. "Thank you. I can see you are troubled." Neeya nodded receptively, knowing he meant it as he sat beside her.

"My name is Emmanuel. I come here several days each week to ponder on life's deeper issues."

"My name is Neeya. Seems I have plenty of life issues these days." It was easy to admit this to him, though it pained her to be so obviously troubled.

"That's apparent." He gently suggested, "Perhaps there is really only one life issue, and all other issues are an expression of that one."

"Well, that would make it simple, Emmanuel. What is that one life issue?" Neeya was surprised how long he paused before responding, peering deeply into her eyes.

"The one issue above all others is when we are not truly in touch with our essential nature, our own true self, our soul."

"Oh. No way I can deny I have that problem! That's one of the reasons I came here today, to see if I can get in touch with whatever is real inside me. Feels like I'm out of touch with it. I used to think of it as the place my conscience comes from."

Emmanuel's smile flowed from his heart. He remained silent, allowing Neeya to continue her inner process if she chose to do so here beside him now. *I think this man has a heart full of love and a ton of wisdom. Makes me feel like an open book. He doesn't even know me but seems to understand me. Feels okay to let him read my book. This is strange, but good. I hope he has something I need to hear.*

"I stopped coming to church to find answers a long time ago," Neeya admitted. "It became too hard to relate to all that ancient biblical stuff. It just didn't explain the answers to my questions about what God is, how it all works, what spirituality is." *Is it okay to be so honest about this stuff with him?*

"Yes, it is, Neeya," he replied, as if knowing what she was thinking. "Please continue."

"Here's another example. See the painting of you-know-who over there, bloody and dying on a cross? How could I feel devoted to an image like that? I mean, it doesn't give out any spiritual type of vibe at all, at least not for me. Why don't they show him alive, with a loving aura or something more pleasant?"

Emmanuel nodded, agreeing. "Christianity surely could have used another image." But he did not want to elaborate or debate her.

She had another question from way back when she was a teenager. *Maybe he can answer this one.* "Emmanuel, there is a line, I guess it's in the Bible, which says something like, 'Jesus was a high priest in an order.' What is that about? I used to wonder. No one seemed to actually know."

Emmanuel answered slowly. "You might consider that he was part of a group, a network of saintly people, ones who could entirely express their divine nature—part of what I might call a spiritual hierarchy, not of authority but of levels of consciousness, of spiritual awareness, of soul."

"Oh. That sounds possible, I guess."

Continuing, Emmanuel explained, "Some people say he was involved with the Essenes, an esoteric priesthood, and that he was a high priest of this group. He spurned the religious leaders of the time, basically accusing them of being out of touch with Truth. Maybe there has always been a small group of people in touch with Truth."

I'm definitely not gonna ask him the classic question, "What is Truth?" That would just be too weird.

Seeing Neeya's openness to what he was saying, Emmanuel continued. "The way I see it, he was an example of what is ultimately achievable for a human being. He basically said it's possible to work on your spiritual development, eventually reaching that same level."

"Me?" she asked him incredulously.

With a big grin, Emmanuel said, "Yes, Neeya, even you."

There was silence for several minutes as Neeya pondered the ramifications of what she had just heard. "What about the spiritual network you mentioned? What is that? It kinda sounds like sci-fi."

"It has always existed, Neeya, mostly in higher realms of consciousness. It's where our greatest human beings come from, people like Mohammed, Moses, Buddha, Leonardo da Vinci, Mother Teresa, Martin Luther King Jr., Joan of Arc, Gandhi, and others we've never heard of who work behind the scenes. In the life which made them famous, many may not have remembered their connection to the inner network, yet they are part of it—the benevolent group which supports and inspires humanity, people who are the expression of the accumulated wisdom of the ages."

Emmanuel grinned again. "They are like a bridge between our physical world and the spiritual realm. And we can cross that bridge too. They are guides along the way, Great Souls, many of whom have mastered life and seek to share that wisdom with us."

"We could sure use some of that help now, Emmanuel."

"True. But until then, we have to help ourselves. We can find the inspiration deep in our own souls. We can figure out how to live, how to make a difference, how to make our lives worthwhile, how to serve the common good."

"That sure is inspiring," Neeya replied. "It's getting in touch with the source of that inspiration and staying connected to it which is a totally major challenge for me."

"It's inside of you, Neeya. It's worth the uphill, long-term, strenuous effort to stay connected to your inner essential being. It is transformative. This may sound impossible, but one approach is to let go of everything else that gets in the way."

Neeya nodded, uneasy about the enormous challenge of such a task yet grasping what he meant and being open to the possibility. She felt receptive to all Emmanuel was saying, since it didn't seem to contradict the Christianity she had learned when younger. It was a deeper explanation, one for a modern humanity.

Neeya remembered her recent dream about what she still liked to call the council of Jedi Knights from *Star Wars*. What Emmanuel described just made it become more believable. *Could I have dreamed about a group that really exists?*

Neeya decided to ask him one last question. "So, Emmanuel, what is heaven?"

"It is the realm where our souls live. It's where we come from and where we will return when our bodily life is over. We can be in touch with it now, however, here on earth." Then, softly, with deep humility, he told her, "I know this from my own experience."

She was in awe, seeing he meant it. Even though Neeya could not confirm it was true, she was not troubled to hear it. *I can't really prove what he's telling me is true, but if I ever met anybody who knew, it would be a man like this, oozing kindness and so clearly full of wisdom. And I just don't pick up any kind of ego trip from him. I may be crazy to believe him, but I guess I do. And he seems to be totally sane too.*

The conversation came back down to earth as they chatted a bit about more worldly matters. They spoke of meeting there in the chapel again but did not make a plan. Neeya placed her hands on his shoulders, thanking him profusely for his wisdom and support. He gave her another smile full of love, saying not a word. Silence sufficed.

Neeya headed home. Her mission to avoid the rabbit hole of depression and find peace was fulfilled.

Neeya checked her voicemail when she arrived back at her apartment to find a message from Hank, pleading for forgiveness and asking to see her. After the briefest pause, she firmly pressed delete. Neeya felt good about doing so. *Yes! I just avoided one of those rabbit holes. It feels so good to know I am letting go of the past and getting ready for the future. Now I just have to create it, and I know I can!* Her mood was definitely getting better.

As Neeya was preparing her lunch, she turned on the news, again avowing that she would not let bad news bring her down. It was to be yet another challenge for her. In Wisconsin, during a debate of candidates running for Congress, a brawl broke out in the audience between far-right conservatives and a group of liberals. There were injuries, but what disturbed her the most was seeing the anger and hate toward others who simply had differing views.

The next story brought news that inflation was now running at 20 percent. The correspondent was interviewing an elderly middle-class woman who began to cry as she described being a widow, living on a limited fixed income, and only being able to afford one meal a day.

There were fewer options at the grocery stores because of supply chain issues, which had only been getting worse in the last year. Neeya was ready to cry herself.

Okay, I can handle maybe one more of these disturbing news stories, and then I'm putting on some feel-good music! I'm not gonna let myself get majorly bummed out before I meet up with Zune for dinner tomorrow. She tried not to think of him as a romantic possibility but was definitely intrigued, wanting to get to know him more.

Well, the next story featured an interview with a woman who was the head of an international interfaith organization. She expressed concerns about the growing loss of faith so many people were experiencing. A deteriorating economy, extreme weather disturbances due to global warming, plus the toxic levels of mistrust and hate were just a part of what was contributing to the disappearance of the middle class and the desperation of those less fortunate. Many blamed God for letting this happen.

What in the world are we doing to this planet? And how the heck can an ordinary person like me do something useful? Even if I made a great video that goes viral, would it actually make a difference? Answers were not yet clear to Neeya, inducing a most uncomfortable feeling. Although she successfully prevented her mood from entering a downward spiral, it did not prevent her from feeling distraught over how bad things had become and how it was looking like things would get worse before they got better. Neeya turned off the TV just before coverage of the collapse of the government in France and two civil wars in Central Africa.

Neeya decided to take a risk and cruise social media to see what people were saying on X, Reddit, Facebook, and Instagram. This provided her with more distress about the state of the world. Despite several insightful posts about the problems in the world and their causes, not only was there next to nothing about solutions, but also, so many messages were filled with hateful, vitriolic tomes, making her begin to feel sick to her stomach.

It had already been a long day, even though it was only early afternoon. Neeya suddenly felt drained physically, emotionally, and mentally. She plopped down on her couch, flat on her back, her head caressed by a pillow, and soon drifted off to sleep.

Neeya found herself in a large, round room with blue marble walls radiating a light of their own. The air was bathed in luminous, cerulean hues. A tall, domed glass ceiling revealed a million scintillating stars pervading a deep, indigo firmament. The oval mahogany table in the center of the room, inlaid with mystical turquoise geometric symbols, seemed familiar to Neeya.

Slowly materializing were the shapes of seven people in chairs around the table, with one chair left unoccupied. Dressed in varying attire, they emitted a rich, rosy aura, permeating the room, warming her heart. Appearing to represent all human races, the palpable unity of this group gave Neeya the impression they were of one mind and one heart.

Neeya couldn't quite make out what they were saying. She soon realized they were communicating without speech. Neeya could hear fragments of what they were thinking—something about concrete solutions offered to support the stability of our civilization. This activity of theirs is part of an ages-long effort to guide and enhance the advancement of humanity. She wondered who was going to fill the empty seat. Then it all slowly dissolved and disappeared.

Neeya awoke feeling this profoundly uplifting scene was a gift she was allowed to witness. She thought the dream was real, or at least a glimpse of some real event. *Either way, maybe it doesn't matter. I was there, and this "there" is real, somewhere. Oh my, there's gotta be no coincidence this dream happened on the same day I met Emmanuel in the church!*

As beautiful as all this was, Neeya again thought, *Okay, wonderful, but what am I supposed to do about all that stuff? Why would I be having a dream like this, leaving me thinking it was actually happening somewhere?* Neeya made a continuous effort to divert her attention and avoid thoughts of futility. She was able to do well enough with this to not get forlorn again while holding on to the experience of the dream. Neeya still vividly felt the aura of benevolence emanating so strongly in that blue room. *Maybe I can go there again…maybe in a dream, maybe for real…*

When Zune invited her to meet up that day, Neeya enthusiastically agreed. *I don't know what he really wants. Same for me, so that makes it easier to say yes and meet him. Lunch at an outside café on the edge of a lake sounds lovely and pretty innocuous. Besides, I need some company that's good for my soul. Romance and intimacy can come some other time, maybe…or, well, okay—hopefully.*

The outdoor patio of the Lake Café was surprisingly close to the water. Neeya could smell its fresh, moist aroma mingling with the jasmine flowers trellised over the patio. She arrived first and could have easily sunk into a restful revelry, noticing a bright-blue indigo bunting in a blossoming bush beside her. Eyes closed, Neeya listened to the hum of honeybees drinking the nectar of purple wisteria flowers just an arm's reach away.

Zune appeared right on time, accompanied by his friend Amara who lived in a renovated loft near Central Park. She had moved there eight years ago from a village outside Beirut, Lebanon, just west of a narrow mountain range running parallel to the coast along the Mediterranean Sea. Zune introduced the two women. They both found themselves liking each other very much right away.

After some pleasant conversation allowing the three companions to get to know each other a bit, Neeya was surprised to find herself wanting to reveal a little about her dream of the benevolent blue room and the encounter with Emmanuel. These experiences had triggered some deep questions within her mind. Neeya hoped Zune, and possibly Amara, had enough wisdom to share some meaningful insight which could help her put it all into perspective. Amara had mentioned she was Muslim with interest in the Sufi tradition, of which Neeya knew almost nothing. Amara appreciated learning Neeya had read some poems by the Sufi poet Rumi and liked the playful twist coloring his reverent writings.

Neeya soon felt brave enough to tell Zune and Amara about Emmanuel and his description of what she called "some kind of network of enlightened beings." Since neither of them raised an eyebrow as they heard this, Neeya felt comfortable asking if they thought such a thing was possible. Both nodded affirmatively. Neeya exhaled, her sigh almost imperceptible, heard only by the chirping bunting just a branch away.

Neeya asked, "So what do you think is actually possible for a human being? How much can a person evolve? How much so-called spiritual growth?"

"Is there anyone from history, or who you ever heard of, who may have reached a point of maximum human potential?" Amara replied.

"I don't really know. There are famous religious leaders like Krishna or Muhammad, and characters in books and movies. I keep thinking of *Star Wars*'s Jedi Knights as an example, but that's a movie."

Zune chipped in here with "Maybe those books and movies have some basis in reality, Neeya."

"That would be cool, for sure!" she responded.

Amara explained, "If you take a look at most spiritual teachings, you'll see they say we have a divine nature and we are encouraged to express it, and it's possible for just about anybody to do so." Neeya wondered how anyone could get fired up enough to spend enough time to try and actually succeed. Neeya joked about having to spend the rest of her life meditating in a cave in the Himalayas to be able to do it.

Zune then told the tale of a man from England who'd spent seventeen years meditating in a Tibetan mountain cave, thinking he had reached enlightenment. When he came back into the world, driving a car in London, he got caught in a massive traffic jam, became impatient, and lost his temper when another driver cut him off. Neeya laughed as she got the message.

Neeya took a risk and told them about her intense dream of the blue room with its glowing light, the wonderfully benevolent vibe coming from the seven people, and the one empty chair. She confided, "It felt like a glimpse into something real and actually happening. For some reason, I was granted a special privilege to be there." *Wow, there it is! I hope they don't think I'm crazy or delusional to believe something like this.*

Zune suggested there a few people like those ones and that yes, maybe Neeya really was there. Amara affirmed such people really did exist and are able to be contacted on the rarest of occasions. That made Neeya chuckle, but inwardly, she found herself believing that those people in her dream really were some kind of Jedi Knights. *That special vibe I felt, filling the room with all that wonderful energy—was that the Force? Oh man, this is getting weird.* Neeya felt a stirring in her soul. It was a kind of reassurance she was on the right track, wherever it leads.

What followed was a discussion about evolution. Perhaps it was both biological adaptation and intelligent design. This made sense to Neeya. Then she asked them, "What about spirituality; how does that fit in?"

Zune responded, "Well, if you believe we are actually souls born into a body, it brings up the question, Where did we come from? Why were we born? How do we live? And what happens when we die? Now consider that we have the potential to live as the soul, not just the personality which develops in this life. The soul is a spark of…well, let's call it a part of something eternal. Suppose you are able to adjust your personality so that little gets in the way and you can fully express your essential essence with whatever qualities and purpose it has?"

"That's really heavy stuff, Zune," Neeya exclaimed. Even so, it seemed possible but brought up hints of reincarnation and karma, which was way too much for her to digest at this point. Neeya's mind was already juggling some new, profound ideas, and she didn't think there was room to manage any more right now. She was quiet for a while. Neeya was slowly coming to the realization, *Yes, the dream truly was real, but I don't need to figure out how just yet.* She remained quiet and reflective.

Amara noticed the vividly blue bird and told them about a bird in the Middle East called the Palestine sunbird.

Neeya had drifted inward and suddenly realized Amara had just called her name, drawing her back into the conversation. Amara looked at her very directly and said, "All of this is fascinating and true to whatever extent you can verify it for yourself, but what really counts is what you do with your life, Neeya. It's about being true to yourself, and that's Self with a capital *S*. It's about what impact your life has on the world, even if it is so very, very small. We all leave some kind of impressions from what we think, feel and do. It affects others and the planet itself. It's also about living our true dream of what we are called to do, if indeed we can hear the calling. That's where meditation comes in. It helps us listen to what we might hear coming from within us."

"Hold on there, Amara! I'm trying to take in all of this. You and Zune just dropped some mind-boggling ideas on me, and I'm trying to process it."

"Take your time, Neeya," Zune advised. "There sure is a lot to consider, and it is incredibly important to think for yourself!"

"Thanks, Zune. Growing up, I was always told we had to just believe the religious stuff we were taught, that it was wrong to question it. A lot of it was awful hard to accept. That was one of the main reasons I drifted away from the church. Excuse me—my mom would say this is a blasphemous question, but if the kingdom of heaven is within, why would I need somebody far away to be some kind of intermediary?"

Amara and Zune smiled quietly again.

"Maybe I don't."

"Why don't you see for yourself, Neeya?" was Amara's sage advice.

"I will," said Neeya humbly. "But first, I have to figure out what to do with my life."

"That's part of the process," said Zune.

Now it was Neeya's turn to smile. "I like that, Zune!"

"Any ideas about what you might do?" Amara asked her.

Neeya told them about her fantasy of crafting a documentary about a solution to a major problem which could be implemented at the local level and become a model initiative shared around the world. She received encouragement from both Zune and Amara to explore this. Neeya expressed her gratitude for their support, though it seemed more than daunting, and she didn't know where to start.

While eating, they chatted about music and food. Amara raved about her mother's falafels, and Zune told a story about his uncle Frank's famous backyard barbecues. When Zune had to leave after lunch, Neeya and Amara agreed to take a walk around the lake. The path was smooth, with soft earth beneath their feet as it slowly curved around the tranquil lake, where wood ducks paddled quietly and turtles rested on rocks. The breeze was gentle and warm. Billowing white clouds floated above, their fluffy whiteness giving a trace of materiality to the infinite depths beyond.

At this point, Neeya was feeling unexpectedly comfortable with Amara, so she decided to further explore her conversation with Emmanuel. Amara listened with interest. As Neeya spoke, the connection between what Emmanuel called the group of Great Souls and the dream of seven benevolent ones in the blue room suddenly coalesced in her mind.

"Oh, Amara! Maybe all this is starting to make sense, starting to come together."

"Did Emmanuel tell you of the common belief among the world's major religions, how they all share an expectation of a messianic figure who is going to appear?"

"Yes, he said something about that. Please go on, Amara."

"Maybe you know this already, Neeya. In Islam, we believe the Imam Mahdi will arrive. The Jews are still waiting for their Messiah. Hindus think Krishna will return, and Buddhists expect Maitreya, the next Buddha. Christians are waiting for the reappearance of the Christ. Even though the religions have different scenarios for where, when, and how this person arrives, it's really amazing that they all have a prophecy of a Coming One! Even the Incan shamans of Peru have a similar prophecy."

Neeya felt goosebumps hearing Amara tell her of the commonly shared expectations. "Gee, Amara, the world sure needs someone like this right now, before this planet of ours goes off the deep end." *Is that why there was an empty chair in my dream of the blue room?*

"We've gotten too close to that abyss, Neeya. Many think we are at that point now and it's time for a Coming One to show up and help humanity figure out how to get back on track."

"From your mouth to God's ears, Amara!" They laughed together, and it felt good.

Neeya continued to wonder about her special dreams, deciding to put it on hold until later when a context for it could emerge more clearly.

Arriving back at the café, their shared hug was truly from the heart. Neeya felt like it was some kind of healing and said so. Amara told her it was simply her mind and heart opening up a little. Neeya knew she was right. After all, the unexpected loss of her job and the breakup with Hank had almost closed the door of her heart. Now she knew it was only temporary, and it was opening again. This was a great relief to her, realizing the darkness of the last few weeks was giving way to a new light. *Maybe it's the light of my own soul.*

CHAPTER

Neeya took a long, slow walk back to her apartment, landing horizontally in her go-to spot, the living room couch. Thoughts of conversations with Amara and Zune filled her mind. Neeya tried to conceptualize what it would be like if there really was a benevolent network of evolved people helping humanity. To do this without putting it into religious terms felt confusing and strange to Neeya. Yet this made it easier, since she didn't have to wrap it around archaic beliefs which now felt like a fairy tale in this modern, digital age. She tried to avoid falling back on the *Star Wars* metaphor, which had provided a sense of comfort given how much she was stretching her previously limited exposure to all this. Still, she kept going back to, *What do I do with my life now?* The uneasiness from a lack of clarity almost undermined the high Neeya felt from her time with Zune and Amara. *I should call Kim. She always helps me get my head on straight.*

Neeya called Kim and shared all that had gone on in the last couple of weeks: the struggle not to get crushed by betrayal and despair, Grace's talk on goodwill, her profound dreams, running into Zune again, meeting Emmanuel at the church, talking with Amara and Zune, and of course the "What do I do with my life now?" piece.

Kim simply listened as Neeya quickly ran through all this, sharing the emotions, inspiration, and discombobulated thoughts accompanying her narrative. Kim empathized with Neeya. "Hey, girlfriend, that sure sounds like some kinda intense, fork-in-the-road crisis!" Neeya laughed, agreeing with Kim. When Kim asked if maybe there was even just one thing which she had been thinking about doing, even if it didn't make sense, Neeya instantly blurted out, "Make that darn documentary!'" Having heard herself say it aloud, she knew she had to do it, even though she still had no idea how or where to start. Kim was totally supportive, and Neeya loved her for this.

"I wish one of those benevolent folks from the blue room would just tell me what to do and how to do it."

"That's way too easy, Neeya, and it's not going to happen. Hey, I'm all for some cosmic intervention stuff, but when it comes down to the most important things in life, we have to figure it out ourselves, and we can."

It felt weird to hear herself agreeing with Kim out loud, affirming, "I know you are right, Kim." Knowing she really did believe it was an empowering realization for Neeya. By the time the two women finished what turned out to be an almost-two-hour conversation, Neeya was feeling pretty good—still somewhat confused, but it didn't bother her now.

Later, just before dawn, in the realm of returning from sleep, just before we fully awake and clothe ourselves anew in brain-centered thinking, a clear thought arose in Neeya's mind. Her brother Favian was currently living in Senegal, doing IT work for a nonprofit involved with development projects in western Africa. She could go there and find something related to his work, which could be a great subject for a documentary. Neeya had no plan in mind and very little knowledge of Africa, but there was no resistance inside her to this sudden idea, and it felt right.

Although Neeya and Favian were very close growing up, they didn't have much in-person contact in recent years. She had not seen him since he'd gone to Senegal. She called him, and he was thrilled to hear her voice.

Favian had invited Neeya to visit him there last year, but it seemed like a fantasy to Neeya then, as Africa was far away in more ways than one.

"So Favian, is your offer to visit still good?" Neeya inquired.

"You bet it is, sis!"

The siblings reveled in the idea of being together in Senegal, so far from home. Neeya felt a visceral expansiveness as she envisioned herself on the edge of the Senegal peninsula, listening to West African music, talking late into the night with her bro. In just a few minutes, they had a plan for a visit, and when Neeya hung up, she sensed a renewal awaiting. She sprung into the new day with an enthusiasm not felt in months.

Cleaning her apartment, Neeya put on some music Favian had sent her. The West African music of Baaba Maal was rhythmic, upbeat, and trancelike, perfectly designed to keep Neeya in a happy, active mode while she dusted, vacuumed, and did a load of laundry. Her passport was still valid, she had saved almost all of her severance pay, and she had a free place to stay in Senegal, and now this out-of-nowhere trip was a real possibility, one that she intended to activate. Plans for the trip materialized very quickly.

A week later Neeya was on her way eastward across the Atlantic. As the earth fell away beneath her, the wings of the Jet Africa plane carried Neeya steeply aloft into the evening sky. She turned her focus to Favian, delighted they will soon be together in Senegal. With more than two years having elapsed since they had seen each other, Neeya missed him dearly. Favian had always been there in the role of big brother, protective and supportive, challenging her, and above all, sharing his brotherly love. They always joked they were sister and brother to the end.

I just want to reconnect and spend some time with him, even if it's only for ten days. He knows his way around and can show me what I need to know. It was the natural way for Neeya to think today—to just leave it all up to Favian.

Neeya eagerly tried the airline's dinner option, featuring food typical of Senegal. She enjoyed it, even if one dish was a little too spicy. The flight attendants were dressed in traditional garb. When she plugged in the earphones and chose to listen to some African drumming, Neeya could not help but find herself feeling excited. *Senegal, here I come!*

Neeya didn't sleep much on the plane. It was a bright, clear, early sunny morning as the plane began its descent toward the very western tip of the African continent. Gazing out the window, the earth was naught but blue, the vast and rippled expanse of ocean covering its surface in all directions. As the plane banked into a steep curve, Neeya's view took in the entire peninsula where the capital city of Dakar sat, awaiting her arrival. She was taken aback by the beauty of the beaches along the coast. They gave way to a mainland which was green just outside the dense city, quickly becoming dry, dusty brown brush inland.

Security was tight. It seemed like forever before Neeya cleared customs. As she passed through the gate, sure enough, there was Favian waiting for her, his broad smile as bright as his red African shirt.

Favian was ecstatic to see Neeya. He began speaking rapidly about all the things they could do and places they would go. "I'm going to give you the royal treatment, sis," Favian assured her. Neeya was completely fine with that. Her life had been seriously challenging lately. She was ready to forget about any woes, simply wanting to be with Favian and enjoy herself, no matter what they did.

They took a taxi to Favian's apartment in Dakar, and right away, Neeya felt comfortable there. It was modest and clean, with traditional West African decor and style. Neeya had never seen most of the plants and trees before, leaving her in awe of this new environment. What really got to her the most were the pungent fragrances of the local flora. The aromas infusing each breath incited her senses, diving deep into her essence. She felt so alive here, even after the all-night flight.

After a bite to eat and a chance to freshen up, Favian and Neeya took a taxi heading northeast, just up the peninsula from Dakar. Beyond the outskirts of the city, they walked through a dry, wooded area and then across the sands to a narrow beach at the ocean's edge.

"So Favian, tell me what it really is like for you here, so far from home."

"Yes, I am so far from home, Neeya, but this place already feels like a second home to me." He paused, turning to face Neeya, looking right into her eyes with real sincerity. "Sure, I miss you, and even Angela too. I miss many things about America and back home. But Neeya, I am happy here, and I am content."

"That's so great, bro!" Neeya was truly happy to see Favian doing so well here in Senegal. "What about your job, Favian?"

"Neeya, I am definitely doing what I like. I am really into developing and implementing computer networks—administering the systems, helping facilitate people's ability to get in touch with each other, making all kinds of communication and information flows possible. Makes me feel really useful." Neeya was pleased for Favian, though she felt a bit envious. "Outside of Dakar, it gets rural really quickly. There is not the level of infrastructure and connectivity we see in more developed nations, even here in the capital. Some government agencies have been able to do their own thing, but the central government does not always have a handle on what's going on throughout the country," explained Favian.

"I am working as a consultant, helping several nongovernmental organizations get connected to the internet and each other, setting up their networks. One of the groups is a collective of farmers growing peanuts and millet, food people really need since they do not have the greatest climate for agriculture here. It can get super dry some years. Helping these folks organize so they can communicate with each other and with governmental departments gives them a chance to survive, to feed people, to not become victims of private traders who may try to buy their products at next to nothing. Do you see? Working here, helping people, makes me feel worthwhile, like I am doing something meaningful."

Neeya walked silently beside Favian along the warm sand. The foamy waves, striving to reach the dunes beyond, caressed her bare feet. Favian's words struck her deeply, and it seemed selfish to feel envious. Favian was living his ideal, and he was happy. It contrasted so sharply with her own life—its lack of direction, her lost boyfriend, lost job, and an unrealized aspiration of doing something enjoyable and worthwhile.

Neeya stopped walking, turning to face the vast, azure ocean. In her heart, she knew the possible paths for her life were as endless as the waves rising and falling before her. *I guess it's time to choose, time to overcome my fears, time to be bold enough to do what I really want, to not let myself down, to really go for it!*

Neeya told Favian of her aspiration to travel to flash points around the globe where critical issues were unfolding in their own crucibles. It wasn't just the idea of making the documentaries that excited Neeya. She envisioned they would be respected and viewed by millions, especially for their practical usefulness. Their poignancy would inspire people to take action. *Grandiose, yes, and it's probably already been done hundreds of times, but maybe I can!*

"What do you have in mind, sis?"

"Well, here's one idea I just heard about, bro. It's about the Sarvodaya Shramadana initiative in Sri Lanka. *Sarvodaya* means awakening of all, and *shramadana* means to donate effort. It was started by a guy named Dr. Ariyaratne. People say he is almost like another Mahatma Gandhi. He encouraged small, poor communities to organize and work together to meet their basic needs. Then communities started cooperating with other communities, building supportive, interdependent systems. He has won all kinds of international awards. I checked him out on YouTube. I mean, this guy was like a saint! He's gone now, though."

"It's truly amazing. There are almost fifteen thousand villages involved. Women and men learn how to motivate and organize people in their own villages, working together to ensure basic human needs are met, like food, a clean drinking-water supply, housing, sanitation, fuel, health care, and education. People are taking care of each other, doing it essentially without help from the government. What's really cool is that this was created while a civil war was raging inside the country and the majority of people were left to fend for themselves."

Favian thought it sounded a bit much for her to accomplish but respected her excitement and gave her some encouraging feedback. He wondered aloud if that kind of documentary was already made. Neeya agreed it was quite possible, saying, "Yeah, I'll have to check it out," though she was afraid to really do so. *Maybe he is right.*

The two siblings spent the next couple of days reconnecting, reinvigorating their special bond as Favian took her out into the countryside and into the older sections of Dakar, where Neeya could experience firsthand the feel and flavor of western Africa. The aromas, colors, sounds, and warmth of the people deeply impressed themselves upon a receptive, adventurous Neeya.

Neeya and Favian had dinner at an outdoor café with his special friend Theo, who he'd met while working on a project with Water for the World, a nonprofit organization based in Geneva. Favian knew Neeya would be intrigued by Theo. He held a high-level administrative position with the United Nations Commission for Refugees.

"Theo is a totally dedicated and busy guy, Neeya. The project with water is a side job in addition to all his work with refugee camps in several nations here in Africa."

Neeya was struck by the dignity emanating from this well-spoken, handsome, charismatic, yet gentle man. She liked the sound of his African accent.

Well, I'm a million miles from home now. It feels like anything is possible. I never could have imagined I would be eating dinner outside under a baobab tree, so far from whatever the heck my life was. Maybe the universe has something up its sleeve for me. I sure hope so!

Over a tasty fish-and-rice dish of *thieboudienne*, Neeya listened attentively as Theo spoke about overseeing a nearby project.

"With drip irrigation, Senegal's farmers can grow crops year-round. Drip irrigation means bigger yields by as much as five times. Farmers pay half as much for water as they did when they used watering cans," Theo explained.

"So you are really helping to meet the basic needs of these people, aren't you?" Neeya inquired.

"Yes, Neeya, that's exactly what we are trying to do."

"Is it the kind of project that can sustain itself after the agency finishes its work there?"

"Good question, Neeya. Projects often fail after a couple of years when the NGOs initiating their projects leave and stop managing them directly—for instance, when something breaks down or if there isn't money for staffing or the community can't agree on how to cooperate and share expenses."

"I bet that happens a lot," Neeya interjected.

"Unfortunately, you're right. With our new initiative, individual farmers are each responsible for their own plot. They pay their own expenses, including water and maintenance costs, but they also get all the profit. The plots are grouped together so the farmers can share technical assistance, crop marketing, and a water source. If this project works, people will have money to buy rice and vegetables. That's why it's so important."

Neeya's eyes opened wider, revealing her enthusiasm as she told him, "I try to stay informed about what's happening around the world but really don't have a heck of a lot of knowledge. Most people in the so-called developed countries are pretty isolated from the reality others experience, especially in developing nations. I mean, is there anywhere else in the galaxy besides the USA where you can see a bumper sticker that says, 'Shop till you drop'?"

"Twelve years ago, I went to a conference in Tokyo and got to meet the man you told Favian about, Dr. Ariyaratne, the one who started the Sarvodaya movement."

"Theo, that is so cool!"

"It *was* really cool, Neeya. He was the most extraordinary man, probably under five feet tall, a totally gentle human being who radiated a profound humility."

"What really amazes me in hearing this, Theo, is that such a gentle little guy could make such large-scale things happen," Neeya added.

"What is so ultimately impressive about this is that on one hand, the movement is so practical, meeting the basic human needs of everyday life. Yet on the other hand, it is the manifestation of a deeply beautiful spiritual philosophy," said Theo.

"Sure sounds like it," chimed in Neeya. "I know this sounds naive and starry-eyed, but hey, if we just practiced the Golden Rule all around the world, what a different place it could be."

"What a different place it *will* be, Neeya."

"I am not sure how we'll get there, but I know you are right, Theo."

It was Favian who added, "It is up to the people to make the great changes which occasionally happen in society or in a civilization. Change must come from the people. Then the governments will follow. Like Gandhi said, 'Be the change.'"

"That is probably true, bro. But I also believe the old axiom, 'Where there is no vision, the people perish.' Someone or some group has to have the vision. Somebody incredibly special has to articulate it for the masses. Then we can become inspired to make those changes on a global scale."

"Whoa, sis, now you're getting pretty deep," uttered her brother. "Sounds like you are talking about some kind of Messiah person like you mentioned. I don't know about that. Last time it happened, the guy got nailed."

Theo then spoke softly yet seriously. "Yes," he agreed. "However, there is another simple and more likely possibility. A network of extraordinarily great leaders will emerge and point out what is possible for humanity. They will indicate to us ways we can deal with our crises and go forward, Great Ones who will deeply inspire enough of humanity to make efforts enabling us to get our act together. And there will be the most special Great One who will show us we really are one human family, one global village, and it's up to us to take care of each other. Followers of the major religions will tell you this has happened before, and they all believe a Great One will appear again." Neeya got the chills.

Theo continued, asking, "Hey, folks, what do you think such a person would be talking about if he showed up tomorrow?" After a pause, Theo continued. "I bet he would tell us to quit solving conflicts with violence, feed the hungry, and transform our economic and political systems to reflect what we really know in our heart of hearts: we are all interconnected in one human family, and it's high time for us to live accordingly."

"Gee, Theo, now you're sounding like a preacher," Favian exclaimed.

Theo elaborated. "I have a sense that great changes are coming, and these changes are imminent. I can do my part to help make it happen. This idea about a great leader or teacher may sound very far-fetched, but it has the ring of truth in it for me. So many folks have ideas about Armageddon and the Rapture and all that, but I wonder. My guess is that things may get worse before they get better. Even so, I will give you my own prophecy based on intuition and an experience I had. We are close to a new era of goodwill in the world, a Great One is on the way, and he—or she—is coming, with their colleagues."

"Ahh!" voiced Neeya. "Thank you so much, Theo, for sharing that. It's a beautiful vision, and the way you tell it makes me think it can really happen. Theo, you're either a real prophet or…I better not say," Neeya wondered aloud.

"Okay folks, just chill," urged Favian. "Now that we've heard a fanciful prophecy and solved the problems of the world, let's get out of here and walk off the tasty dinner we just had." His two companions agreed. They went for a walk along a beach near Malika, where the ocean's deep sapphire undulated toward them only to be drawn back again to its rolling depths by waves moving in both directions.

Upon returning to Favian's apartment, Theo went back to his hotel while Neeya decided to take a short stroll around the neighborhood.

She was feeling too excited to go inside yet. Favian told her not to eat anything from the local vendors' stalls, since her stomach was not used to handling the bacteria she was likely to encounter. The locals had grown up with it, so their systems managed well.

Strolling past the small shops and food carts, Neeya abided by her brother's warning, avoiding food she could not be certain was prepared in a manner that killed the microbes which could potentially wreak havoc with her guts. She was thirsty, though, from the spicy, salty fish and figured it would be okay to have a small cup of lemonade from a clean-looking stall. It went down fine.

Soon after, Neeya was back at her brother's apartment on a comfortable cot in Favian's living room. Before drifting off into a deep sleep, Neeya thought, *Well, maybe if I really try to do something meaningful with my life, the right opportunities will emerge. Yeah, effort meets future in a place called fate. Hmm…*

The next day, their plan was to visit a village a few hours east of Dakar where Neeya could shoot some video interviews with local millet growers about their drip irrigation project. They would go to the city of Kaoloack to meet a farmer named Demba. He will take them to see progress he and other local millet farmers had made with methods Water for the World had developed. It sounded like a great idea to Neeya, especially as Theo would be joining them.

Theo explained, "Demba knows that soon it will come time for Water for the World to leave, and they need to be sure farmers do not become dependent on international development aid. Yes, Demba is grateful for the help, accepting it because it is a tool toward becoming fully independent as farmers had been for many generations while barely eking out a subsistence living on the arid land. For Demba, there is much personal and national pride involved. He is a Moslem of the Tijani Sufi order, believing that by succeeding in his farming, his ability to make the mystical connection with his beloved creator would be strengthened.

"The deserts are expanding, consuming the farmland. Demba believes he has been given the mission of countering the troubling forces of nature by bringing water to this increasingly parched earth and ensuring the people of Senegal are fed."

Neeya began to have trouble paying attention. An uneasy, queasy feeling was developing in her stomach. She did not want to believe she was getting sick, but she was, and other sensations were happening lower down.

"Excuse me," Neeya abruptly uttered as she jumped up and headed quickly for the bathroom. Theo rightly assumed by the look on her face that this was a GI situation. For the next twenty-four hours, Neeya suffered through a bout of diarrhea and vomiting, essentially immobilizing her. She was drained the following day, only able to drink fluids. It was not until the third day that she felt almost okay yet still weak, leaving her deeply disappointed not to have gone to meet the millet farmers and see their water project.

Only a few days away from going back home, Neeya felt unfulfilled. Her plan to shoot a video in Africa was not going to materialize. She strived to determine what she could do to salvage her need to do something. Neeya kept thinking about Theo's so-called prophecy and how it jived with what Emmanuel had told her that day in the cathedral as well as with her own dreams of those benevolent ones in the blue room. Then an idea arrived in her mind.

Yeah! I can do a ten-minute interview with Theo about his proph-ecy, but I really shouldn't call it that in the video—could sound kinda out there. I don't want to be thought of as some kind of New Age nutcase. This has gotta be mainstream.

Neeya was gleefully surprised Theo agreed to do an interview. They met up on her last day in Senegal at the outdoor café under the broad baobab tree. Neeya set up two ultra-high-def video cameras Favian had brought and some good microphones, and they were ready to go. She wanted this to be informal, as if they were just chatting. Even so, Neeya was entranced hearing Theo share his thoughts so simply and elegantly. It was the perfect time of day, as the late afternoon sunlight shone just right on his brown face.

After a very brief introduction, avoiding mention of Theo's job with the UN, she asked him just one question about his vision of Great Leaders and the spread of goodwill. They were off and running. Theo spoke lucidly. Neeya was again greatly inspired. The more she consid-ered this Great Leaders idea, the more real the possibility became for her. She tried to remain open to it, as weird or blasphemous as it may have sounded to lots of people.

Working with Favian on his computer, they tweaked the audio and made some simple edits of the camera angles. Neeya soon had a seven-minute video interview completed. *When I get home, I'm gonna find a way to get this thing out there into cyberspace and hope for the best!* This was the first time in months Neeya had felt good about what she had done and, more importantly, felt content with herself.

Before she left for the airport, Neeya had one last visit with Favian and Theo. It occurred to Neeya that she hadn't asked Theo about his main work with the UN refugee program, so she inquired. What Theo explained made Neeya start to feel sick to her stomach again. Millions of people in multiple countries who had been living their lives were suddenly forced to leave home to live in utter squalor far away. They were displaced by civil war, climate disasters, or famine.

Conditions in the camps were often horrible. Families crowded into small tents, which leaked. Many lived under tarps, which sometimes blew off their poles, floating rapidly away in the wind. People usually had only one meal a day, and it was not always fully cooked, as there was little gas fuel to be had. It could take two hours of walking to and from the sparse, arid hills where they could scrounge in the baking heat or the infrequent torrential rains for some branches to bring back to the camp for firewood.

Refugees slept on mats on dirt floors, sometimes shared with bugs, rodents, and snakes. They were dependent on what was left of the help from governments and nonprofit aid agencies. Civil war often made it next to impossible to leave. Illness was widespread. Desperation and despair were the unfortunate themes.

Theo is doing too good a job telling his story. The images I am getting are overwhelming. Is this what I have to do, get stories like this out there in a useful, practical way? I'll figure out how to do it when I get back home.

After effusive goodbyes and heartful hugs, Neeya was soon in a plane heading west across the Atlantic Ocean. By midnight, she was back in her apartment. Easing down onto her beloved couch, she was flooded with recollections of her time in Africa. Neeya was feeling renewed and ready for the next phase of her life, one of her own creation, even if inspiration shared space in her mind with anxious thoughts of failing. *Sure, I could fail, but I can succeed! Yeah!*

9 CHAPTER

Back home the next day, Neeya felt like her trip to Senegal could have been a dream. Yet so much of it remained present with her: conversations with Theo, the warmth of her brother Favian, Africa itself, and the mounting determination to get her video interview with Theo out into the world.

Neeya didn't use social media extensively but knew it was a necessary tool to have as many people as possible see it. She got ready to upload it to Facebook, Reddit, Threads, YouTube, and X. Holding her breath, Neeya affirmed her intention out loud and hit the Submit button. In a few seconds, there it was, ready for all to see. Neeya was cautiously optimistic but also knew it might only be seen by twenty or thirty people. *Either way, I did it, and the video is out there in the public realm! It feels so good to finally take some action on my intention, whatever the results may be.*

After going about her business of eating, reading her mail, and doing a large load of laundry, Neeya went for a long walk in Central Park. She dispensed with thoughts of Senegal and her video, simply moving freely along the paths, soaking in the warmth of the day, hearing the laughter of the children playing, and listening to a woman playing saxophone on a grassy hillside.

After a few errands, Neeya arrived back home, feeling exquisitely relaxed, wanting just to rest, not sleep. Those dark days of Hank's betrayal and the loss of her job were gone, replaced by the start of a new phase of life, vitalizing her with a sense of hope.

Neeya answered her cell phone to the sound of Kim's excited voice. "Hey, Neeya! I just saw your post online and watched your video. It was seriously good, of course, but what is freaking me out right now is that it's been viewed almost three thousand times, and it's only been out there a few hours. You go, girl!"

Neeya was thrilled, though it was hard to believe. She spent the next twenty minutes talking nonstop to Kim, telling her all about her trip to Senegal. Kim shared her excitement and kept voicing support of Neeya's new intentions. Neeya was so grateful for this. "Sometimes I think you're just about the only one who really gets me, Kim." She couldn't see Kim's wide, bright smile. Kim couldn't see Neeya bouncing around the room.

This is really cool, but people are only likely to see my video if they are into stuff like climate change, refugees, or certain kinds of prophecies. How am I ever going to reach a lot of people with a message that will really change how we see things?

Zune had not come to mind much since her walks on the beach in Dakar. Now, Neeya found herself wanting to connect with him and talk about her video. She knew he would be open to hearing about it and hopefully would share some of her excitement. Neeya called Zune, and they made a plan for him to come over for dinner the next day. Neeya was still uncertain what she wanted out of her relationship with him. It was clear that they were simpatico, and she wanted to connect with him more meaningfully.

That night, Neeya had another one of those dreams—a dream of... *Well, I don't know what to call those people. Glowing with energy, telepathic with each other, sending out benevolent vibes...Beings of Light would be a good description*...though she felt awkward to think of using those words to tell others about them. Neeya didn't want people to think she was some kind of wacko channeling mystical spirit guides who cruised around the astral plane, blowing kisses to us.

This time was different though. She could tell—or was someone there telling her?—each of these seven people was working in a different field of modern life. They were sending out insight and concrete ideas to address significant problems. Neeya began to actually see their streams of thought become available to the minds of people around the world, people working in areas of politics, education, business, science, the arts, and more. It felt to Neeya as if they had all the bases covered. *Maybe this is how people get some of their creative ideas and inspiration.* She remembered Beethoven supposedly said he occasionally would suddenly hear an entire symphony in his head, then write it down and get credit for composing it. *I should call them the Seven Muses,* Neeya thought to herself.

Then the scene shifted, and the Seven Muses turned their attention to the empty chair waiting to be filled. Suddenly, Neeya became aware of a radiant, golden glow, and it felt wonderful. It looked like living liquid light. It began to vaguely take shape, though it had no face or solid form. *Surely it is somebody. What else could it be?* As a wave of love washed through her, Neeya felt as if something divine was present here. She didn't know exactly what *divine* meant, *but what else could fill my heart with all this love?*

Whoever, or whatever, had filled the empty chair rayed out seven streams of energy, each one a different color. Each of the Muses absorbed and transmitted one of the seven rays out into the world. Neeya could see that they used the rays of energy in their own fields of endeavor. The one who filled the empty chair and provided the energy was acting like a prism. *Maybe he is a prism. Who knows where he gets that energy from?* She saw the seven colored rays of energy streaming forth from the Prism, then through the Muses and out into the world. Each ray had a different feeling to it. She wondered how she could tune in. *Will I ever find out?*

It was clear to Neeya that the one she now called the Prism had been expected by the Seven Muses. Neeya suddenly felt certain the Muses and the Prism will soon be emerging into public view. How or where, she did not know, but, *They are coming, and it's going to be good. Incredibly good!*

Neeya realized it was time for her to go. She effortlessly drifted away, feeling a sense of true privilege to have witnessed whatever in the world that was. When she awoke, it was all still with her. *How can I ever be the same after that?*

Neeya spent the morning trying to make sense of the dream. Despite her lack of a clear explanation, she knew it was real, or at the very least, a symbol of something real and actually happening. *But if it was real, then maybe it wasn't a dream?* Neeya remembered her recent conversations with Emmanuel, Amara, and Zune. Her mind was spinning as she tried to formulate an understanding. It was obvious to Neeya that she would have to significantly revise her understanding of things spiritual.

Neeya's thoughts kept going back to the Seven Muses. *That's just what the world needs: a group of totally special people who have the wisdom and the energy to help humanity not go off the rails and to get our civilization back to health. We truly do need some profoundly remarkable great leaders. That's it! Great Leaders! That's the video I can make!*

It brought a great sense of relief to come up with this idea herself, not from someone else. *This is why I had the experience, so I would know what I have to do. No matter what the outcome, I just gotta do it. I've never felt so psyched about something so weird as this.* Neeya was fired up and couldn't wait for Zune to get there so she could tell him.

Neeya realized that when Zune planned to come over for dinner, they hadn't agreed on a time, so she picked up her phone to call him. She tried four times, but each time, the call dropped before he answered. Neeya might have let frustration set in if it wasn't for the buoyant state remaining since the latest of her dreams. The new phone she'd ordered three months ago still had not arrived, since a shortage of computer chips had caused a delay. She'd called again last week to find out the phone was either in a container still at a port in South Korea or it was at the LA port waiting for a truck driver to bring it across the continent. Neeya was unable to be given an ETA for the phone.

Neeya laughed to herself, deciding to mentally send Zune a message asking him to call her, imagining he was calling her right now. She shrugged, laughing again when her phone didn't ring.

Half an hour later, the phone rang. It was Zune. *I'll be coming over at seven this evening.* Neeya couldn't resist asking him, "Why didn't you call me earlier, Zune?"

"Gee, Neeya. I was out taking a walk a little while ago when all of a sudden, I got a strong urge to call you, but I hadn't brought my phone with me."

Neeya told him about trying to send him a mental message. "Very cool, Neeya. I guess that's how telepathy works." Hard to prove, yet it was easy for her to agree with him.

Neeya walked over to the local market to pick up a few things for dinner. She was glad to be looking for chicken, since the shelf for meat was nearly empty and the prices were really high. There were no wings or drumsticks, though she was able to find two nice pieces of organic chicken breast going for $14 each. It was slim pickings in the produce aisle too. Neeya encountered several people there bitterly complaining about all kinds of shortages, including paper towels and orange juice.

"Why don't they fix it?" was the exasperated refrain customers repeatedly uttered as she wondered, *Who the heck is it that's actually supposed to fix it? That used to be the government, who I always thought would protect us and ensure our infrastructure worked. Now the government doesn't seem to be working very well. Republicans are too extreme to the right; Democrats are too progressive to the left. The new independent, centrist Middle Path party is too small to make enough difference. Things are so out of control. Disagreement rules. Where are the leaders who can bring us together?*

It was hard for Neeya to believe, but these shortages were increasing every week, and few people were expecting things to get better anytime soon. Many felt it was going to keep getting worse. Neeya began to think of ways she could trim down her lifestyle to keep it simpler, but it felt too disturbing. She shifted her thoughts back to how she would prepare dinner, deciding to be grateful for the food she did have. This intentional adjustment of her perspective was successful. *It is what it is, and sometimes I just have to accept it. Yeah. Okay.*

Around the corner, above a bodega offering sim cards, cell phone accessories, tablets, and other tech supplies, hung a hand-painted sign proclaiming, "No cash—bartering only." Neeya had to stop and reread the sign three times before she could accept what she was seeing. When she inquired what they wanted for a sim card which would fit her phone, the examples were either a five-gallon can of cooking oil or ten pounds of meat. Neeya walked slowly away, stunned by the state of things, realizing that commerce as we knew it was deteriorating before her eyes.

Maybe I should stock up on the basics. Oh crap, then I would just be participating in some kind of panic-buying, which would only make things worse. I could go to the bank and get a couple thousand dollars out just in case, but if money gets replaced by bartering, that won't help. Oh, wow. I'm just gonna take an easy, full breath in, exhale slowly, and hope for the best.

I'd pray, but right now, I'm not sure how or where to direct it. What about the person—or should I say, the being—in the dream, the one I call the Prism? Maybe there's such a one who can hear a prayer? That's easier to imagine than a God who is the universe itself.

Neeya was freaking herself out with these thoughts and couldn't stop them, so she plugged in her earbuds, turning on an oldies station.

By the time she got home, she was humming that old Beatles song, "Let It Be." *Yeah, I'll just let it be. Don't need an answer now.*

Zune arrived promptly at seven. A friendly hello hug lingered, their bodies pressed against each other, hearts warming. Neeya was beginning to feel a new kind of love for—or was it with?—Zune, but it was not like the love she felt for her brother and not like the romantic feelings she has had for several men in her life. It was not merely a physical attraction, either, though she clearly felt that too.

Oh well, I don't have to understand it right now, it's just really so nice, and that's fine with me. I'll figure out this Zune thing later! Zune knew what it was. It did not have to be put into words, at least not now. They both knew there was something for them to do together. It was waiting just ahead, too vague to be tangible yet, and this was okay.

Before Zune could sit down, Neeya began excitedly telling him about last night's dream and her idea for what she called the Great Leaders video. Zune responded with enthusiastic encouragement. *Maybe that's why I like him so much!*

Zune had said very little to her about his Journey on the Infinite Highway of Life. Now, he felt comfortable enough to reveal his intuitive feeling that when he had gone far enough on this Journey, he would be in a place where the world was different, in a good way. Zune avoided predictions about the future, especially given what he was seeing in the world around him these days. He simply told Neeya, "When the future is calling, I must go." She knew what Zune meant yet found it hard to imagine herself setting out on a long journey without a clear destination.

For Neeya, the future was too abstract to be a destination unto itself. For Zune, it was a calling he could not resist. He simply sensed when it was time to go, eventually finding he was at his destination as he arrived. The rest will take care of itself. Ultimately, it was about the journey, not the destination. *The Journey will create the future as I get to the right destinations,* he affirmed to himself.

While Neeya's main course was slow-cooking in the oven, they turned on the news to scenes in Chicago and Philadelphia. There were images of tumultuous rioting in the streets and looting of grocery stores. The out-of-control inflation, coupled with shortages of produce, bread, and meat, had become severe. The worst drought ever in California, where much of the produce consumed in the US was grown, was causing major shortages of fruits and vegetables. Droughts in the Midwest were baking the grain fields, which fed the cows and were used for making bread and pasta. It was the feeling of helplessness and frustration toward the government and Big-Ag for not fixing things that was driving people to lash out. Daily life just wasn't what it used to be. Folks were angry and losing hope.

Zune and Neeya discussed how the deteriorating political situation in the US had become so polarized with partisan antagonism that virtually no important legislation was being passed these days. People were blaming the government, calling it ineffective. Were they right? *Isn't the government supposed to* be *the people?* Despite this ineffective, hateful turbulence, some members of Congress were offering bipartisan plans to actively address the woes, but lately, notes of optimism were getting drowned out by those espousing unwavering, one-sided positions.

Neeya felt a guilty sense of relief as the coverage shifted overseas. More dismay came as they witnessed similar riots in Europe, Africa, and Asia. These were regular people out in the streets looting stores, throwing rocks at government buildings. The plots varied, but the themes were the same: fuel and food shortages, relentless inflation, and new viruses like COVID and Secata Z, which just kept getting worse. In just a couple of years, shortages of workers had turned into shortages of jobs, businesses were closing, and now widespread unemployment had become a major issue. It was a financial crisis, big time.

The coverage shifted back to the US, and the story was alarming. Radical groups from both sides of the spectrum were planning massive protests in front of government buildings in many states. The risk of chaos and violence was increasingly high. Neeya and Zune were deeply perturbed to see how bad things really were.

"How the heck are we going to get out of this mess, Zune? It's a seething vat of chaos out there!"

"Well, Neeya, maybe it will take a handful of those Great Leaders you are talking about. I had a lot of hope that when our first female president, Leeanne Prima, got elected, she would make a real difference. Prima is fiscally conservative, socially kinda liberal, and basically a centrist. She's in the Middle Path party, as you know. That's why she ran as a moderate. It is just incredible that a woman got elected, and she wasn't even a Democrat or a Republican!"

"Yeah. My hope was that she could bring people together, maybe in ways a man hasn't, but that is not happening," Neeya lamented.

Zune was fighting off a feeling of pessimism trying to rear its ugly head. He suddenly remembered Nola, from Bleakville, unable to move beyond her troubles. Zune wondered where she was now. There was again something very familiar about her in Neeya. He could not quite understand it, finding himself staring at her, wondering.

"I just don't see things getting better until people stop being so angry at each other and can coalesce around what there is that we can agree on. Then we can get along well enough to solve the major problems we have in common" offered Zune.

"Yeah. Some people just try to disagree better. That would be progress, but same question; how can people who disagree so intensely work together?"

Zune paused for a couple of minutes. Neeya dismissed a flash of anxiousness, remaining patient in her anticipation of whatever he was about to say.

"So, when I was maybe twelve or thirteen, I saw an old black-and-white movie on TV made around 1950 called *The Next Voice You Hear*. It told the story of a middle-class, blue-collar suburban family—regular folks struggling through everyday life, easily getting annoyed with each other. All of a sudden, one evening, a voice comes on the radio. It's on every radio station all over the world, and everyone listening hears it in their own native language. The voice talks for just a couple of minutes in everyday terms, encouraging people to see others, and themselves, in a more respectful and kind way. People were confused and dubious about the source, but they started mulling over the message. Some people said it was God, but most were unsure what the heck it was. This goes on for six nights in a row. No religious, doctrinal stuff. Just simple wisdom about being kind and helpful, getting along with each other. At least, that's how I remember it.

"What was really cool was that as people began to embrace the messages they were hearing, you see them getting along better with themselves and each other. Distrust and negativity are replaced by kindness. People made the effort to understand each other and, well, to be nice. The world started changing.

"By the seventh day, millions around the world gathered together locally to hear the next message from the voice. But there was only silence. The voice never came on again. It left you feeling, okay, we heard what we needed to hear, we've been inspired to make some changes, and now it's up to all of us to live accordingly."

Zune paused again, as he could see Neeya was taking it all in and processing what she had just heard.

"Zune, that is a wonderful story and really helpful for me. I'll look for it online. I'm psyched about this Great Leaders video, but I am afraid it could end up like some kind of religious prophecy about a savior, and that's not what I intend or expect. The movie you just told me about somehow makes this Great Leaders thing more believable, at least to me. Its people have that to make the changes. Maybe we just need some special inspiration."

"That's why I am telling you this, Neeya. I've kept it to myself, but ever since I saw that movie, I've had a sense that something like it is actually going to happen. Unfortunately, I haven't seen any truly extraordinary, great leaders show up on the scene, but I still hold onto the possibility. My Journey into the future toward as-yet-undetermined destinations may have something to do with it. I think the Infinite Highway will take me there. I just have to keep traveling it. Soon."

Neeya reminded Zune about Emmanuel's description of an extraordinary, esoteric group and how her dreams about the Prism and the Muses were maybe connected to it. He listened attentively.

"So Zune, do you think it's possible that there really is some kind of group or network of advanced, highly evolved beings? Maybe a spiritual kind of thing? Those guys who started religions, could they actually be part of some group? One that still exists? It sounds like New Age sci-fi fantasy, but it would be incredibly cool if it was true."

He looked her right in the eyes and stated it affirmatively, as if he knew. "Yes, Neeya, I do believe something like that exists."

"Oh. Okay. Wow."

"However, 99 percent of what you read about all this stuff is mostly nonsense. Be careful, and trust your own intuition," Zune encouraged her.

"Gotcha."

Over dinner, Neeya and Zune did not feel a need to talk. They were comfortable in the silence. So much had already been seen and heard in the last hour. It was time to digest it all, minimizing any agita or needless rambling.

Later, they talked deep into the night. Neeya was so grateful for Zune's support of her idea for the Great Leaders video. He had several suggestions which she knew were useful.

Zune shared a little more about his Journey on the Infinite Highway, sensing he was heading on a road toward the creation of a more harmonious future. However, in these dark days of conflict, climate crises, pandemics, and crumbling economies, it was sometimes challenging to maintain the vision. At least he knew what it would not be like and that these dark times will soon yield to an era of light. Zune thought initiatives like Neeya's video could be one of many thousands of things making a big difference, sooner rather than later.

"Who sent you, Zune?" she asked him.

"Maybe my destiny sent me."

"Maybe our destiny sent you," Neeya earnestly suggested. *Maybe "they" sent you!*

It was another one of those situations where they both sensed an overlapping, shared destiny. Thinking this could be true made it easier for Neeya to just enjoy their special connection and how nice it felt when Zune was close beside her. *It would be lovely for a romance to evolve*, Neeya thought, though she knew it could also be a booby trap of distraction. Her conscience was at work here, and Neeya had no impetus to ignore it. This made life easier. *Oh well, maybe we'll get intimate a little later. That would be sweet, I'm sure.* She imagined Zune might share a similar sentiment, but there was no way she was going to ask him, remaining unaware he already had to make an effort to keep it platonic.

Neeya awoke in the morning to find herself on the couch embraced with Zune. Other than shoes, they were fully dressed. It felt so good to hold him close. For Zune, it felt nice to spend the hours of sleep with her snuggled up against him, but his determination to soon get back on the road obscured any possibilities. Avoiding any serious physical intimacy with Neeya made this easier.

10 CHAPTER

After Zune left, Neeya was ready to start making some concrete plans for how to make her video. Feeling a need to freshen up her brain, she decided to go out for a short, brisk walk. Neeya passed the building superintendent in the lobby, greeting him with a smile.

"Hi there," he said rather blandly. "I heard from one of your neighbors that you lost your job recently. Sorry, but keep in mind that your rent is still due on time, every month." Neeya was momentarily offended, though she was beyond irritability today after her lovely time with Zune. She nodded and headed outside, avoiding further eye contact.

As she walked, Neeya thought about her sister Angela, feeling like it would be okay if they never spoke again, considering Angela's betrayal with Hank. Still, the other voice in Neeya's head said, *I should be the mature one, even if Angela is older. After all, we are sisters, family, and maybe our bond can outlast her betrayal. It will pain me to call her to tell her about Favian and Senegal, but my conscience tells me it's the right thing to do. Yuck.*

Neeya did call Angela that afternoon. While telling her about Favian, Senegal, and Theo, Neeya reexperienced the wonders of her trip, making it feel fresh and real to her again. They enjoyed speaking with each other about Favian—at least they had that solidly in common.

Neeya hesitantly told Angela about her idea for the Great Leaders video. Angela verbalized some barely sincere support, but when she heard Neeya tell her how she hoped it would have a big impact, Angela laughed, telling her she was grandiose. That was it for Neeya. *She always finds some way to insult me. This will never change, but my relationship with her sure is about to change. She just could not wait to try and burst my bubble. I'm not gonna vent my anger about Hank, because she may enjoy it as some kind of twisted victory. Bye, Angela. I'm going back home now, and I'm gonna sketch out an outline for the Great Leaders story. I'll give it my best, and then whatever happens, happens.*

Over the next few weeks, Neeya immersed herself in searching the internet, tracking down articles about historical figures considered to be great leaders and finding info and video clips about them. After going back and forth for a while, she realized she didn't have the creative juices or the skill to craft a historically focused piece, though she did have enough confidence in her potential to make a good documentary. Neeya began to put together a list of qualities great leaders had. She had no clarity yet how to incorporate her dreams of the Seven Muses and the Prism, but she was determined to do so.

Neeya developed a routine providing enough structure in her daily life so she would not get unnecessarily distracted by people or unexpected situations. There was no resistance at all when the alarm went off at 6:00 a.m. A shower was followed by ten minutes of meditation. Neeya enjoyed whole grain toast with almond butter and honey, washed down with freshly ground, organic, Honduran dark-roast coffee. By seven she was at her desk and raring to go. She usually had enough mental energy and motivation to work straight through until noon. After lunch, if there was a loose end which left her unsettled, Neeya would continue on until she was satisfied with her work. She usually spent afternoons taking care of the business she liked to call *my regular life.*

Her next step was to write a narrative, explaining in simple terms the qualities these great leaders had and how their work makes a real difference in the world. It could be in politics, religion, science, or any other field. Neeya made frequent calls to Zune, who was always available to give her feedback and good ideas. Their bond continued to strengthen. He suggested to Neeya that she was crafting a "videomentary." She had never heard the word before but liked it and started using it.

As the video project soon began to precipitate into form, Neeya realized someone would have to narrate it but had no idea who it might be. Several famous people came to mind, but Neeya knew she would never be able to get in touch, and even if she did, they probably had a hundred other opportunities on their plate. Neeya was stumped.

Neeya decided to call her brother Favian, since they hadn't talked on the phone since she'd left Senegal. It was great to hear his voice, and it always made his day when she called. Neeya told him she was finally working on the video, and he shared her excitement. When she mentioned the need for a narrator, Favian quickly responded "What about Theo?" She immediately loved the idea. "His voice has such deep resonance, and he sounds so kind and strong," she replied. *His African accent is kind of cool too,* she thought.

"Okay, Neeya. I'll reach out to Theo and get back to you. Give me a couple of days since I have no idea where on the planet he is right now. He is big-time involved in lots of projects with the UN and is always super busy."

"You're a darling, bro. That sounds just perfect. Thanks so much!"

They chatted for a few more minutes and then said their goodbyes. Neeya hung up the phone feeling really psyched. She sat on her couch imagining Theo reading the narrative out loud with his deep voice and strong, handsome face. The phone rang about fifteen minutes later.

"Neeya?"

"Theo!" Her heart leapt at the sound of his voice. "Oh my God, I can't believe you're calling me!"

"I am so glad to be calling you, Neeya. I just got off the phone with Favian. He told me about your videomentary project, and it sounds just wonderful. I would love to be a part of it."

"You're a godsend, Theo. I am so thrilled."

Neeya gave him a preliminary description of what his role would be and how to address the technicalities of recording him. A plan quickly emerged. He would do the intro, narrate the main content of the videomentary, and provide the closing comments. The intro and closing would have his face visible on the screen. The whole piece would be about thirty minutes.

Theo understood this project was meant to inspire people to expect, and somehow call forth, great leaders so desperately needed in the world today. Neeya was aware he was very well known due to his high-level position at the UN, and this could help draw a wider audience for the finished product. The best part was when Neeya told him about her dreams of the Seven Muses and the Prism. It sounded very plausible to Theo. He was even willing to agree that, on some level, they were actual experiences of hers. *This is perfect. Thank you, universe!*

Neeya's daily focus now was almost entirely on this project. The Seven Muses and the Prism often came to mind. The more she worked on the documentary project, the more she became convinced these "benevolent ones" were real. Her ten-minute morning meditation had always been basically to relax and get clear. Lately, Neeya was making an effort to reach the ever-elusive source of her inspiration, assuming it was the same source as her conscience, nothing devotional or religious in her approach. Neeya came to realize the source was her own soul. Getting more in touch with it felt like a really good thing to do. Something was luring her deeper within.

Sometimes during her meditation, Neeya would get a fleeting, vivid glimpse of the Muses and the Prism. This fueled her determination. It made her feel uncomfortably humble to think it might be her destiny to make this videomentary. Neeya tried to put her ego aside so she didn't get grandiose, like Angela sarcastically warned.

Neeya soon realized the technicalities of videomentary editing were way beyond her skill level, even after she tried using a highly rated video editing app and watching a few hours of free lessons on YouTube. Her head was spinning. She felt overwhelmed and stuck, knowing she was in way over her head. When Neeya told Zune about this major challenge, he offered to cover the expense of hiring a professional video editor. Neeya was greatly relieved and immensely thankful.

A close-to-final version of the videomentary Neeya was now calling simply *Great Leaders* was almost ready. She was amazed Theo had somehow found the time to help her and be part of the project. After all, he was a UN executive and was busy all over the world. She sent Theo a link to the videomentary, asking if he wanted any edits or if he thought it was ready to go live and be distributed. Neeya had prepared a list of social media sites and other places which might post it. She was feeling very hopeful.

A few days passed, and Theo had not yet responded to her email. Neeya emailed Favian, who reminded her how busy Theo was, advising her to just be patient and wait for him. That was easy for Neeya at first, but when several more days passed with no response, she began to worry. She called her friend Kim, who told her to "just trust the universe and be patient," but it was only helpful for an hour or so. Then the worrying resumed. After a week Neeya was seriously anxious, worried maybe something bad had happened to Theo. She had his phone number but despite the increasing anxiety was too hesitant to directly call this busy man of such high international stature. *Please, please be okay, Theo.*

Three days later Theo finally called. Neeya could tell by the tone in his voice that something was not quite right. Theo explained how Pierre Abara, the assistant secretary general of the UN, had learned he was involved with the videomentary. Abara told Theo such a project was "out of your scope of practice." Theo explained to Neeya that it was virtually a direct order to cease, and certainly a major obstacle. He would be taking a risk to continue working with Neeya.

"I've had to take some time to develop a work-around. That's why I was so delayed in getting back to you, Neeya. Mr. Abara assigned me major budget revisions for every sector in my department with only a week to get it done. I had to work on it every waking moment. That's how he tried to keep me away from your project."

Despite his initial tone of voice, Theo warmly encouraged Neeya to remain optimistic. "Mr. Abara is a totally busy man. He works seven days a week. He oversees much of the general functioning of the UN. And just today, with one new war breaking out at the border of Armenia and Azerbaijan and another war in Africa involving the Congo, this man won't even have time to sleep. He will forget about my help with your project. So I will continue working with you, Neeya."

"God bless you, Theo! I don't know how I can ever repay you."

"You don't have to, and I hope you never try. I'm doing this for the world. Expecting payback is arrogant and selfish."

"Time for another 'God bless you, Theo!'"

"It is my privilege. I am so grateful to have the opportunity to be of service to you and beyond, Neeya. Your dreams may very well portend something imminent. Perhaps extraordinary Great Leaders are coming, and the greatest of them all will emerge too. This is what humanity can really use now!"

"You da man, Theo." His humble laugh preceded hers by a fraction of a second.

Neeya was surprised he had shared his expectation with her. It inspired her, even if it still seemed strange for her to be having these vivid dreams of the Muses and the Prism. *It must be possible they exist, working behind the scenes and now beginning to go public. That has never happened before, has it? Gee, maybe things are so bad we really do need a group like them to show up and provide the kick in the butt humanity needs in order to realize we're all in the same boat, and we need to work together to keep it afloat…or it could sink!*

Neeya imagined what it would be like if a group of extraordinary Great Leaders appeared on the world scene. *How would we recognize them and know their real stature? Would humanity then be able to respond and determine how we get can along with each other and not destroy things through war and pollution? Are they gonna do some miracles? Maybe things really are so bad that not only do we need a messianic-type dude, but we also need a whole group of his colleagues too…? And what if the Prism is a woman? That would be really cool, big-time! Guess I'll just have to wait and see.*

The answer to her ponderings was slowly becoming evident to the public, but not quite as Neeya imagined. Lucia Nuno was a woman living in Spain who'd become the international thought leader of a dramatic overhaul of modern educational systems. Her ideas were widely accepted and implemented, especially in the field of mainstream psychology. She brought forth an acceptable understanding of how the mind is nonphysical, that it does our thinking, and that the brain is its physical instrument which stores and processes data. Given her combination of current scientific research and lucid insight, many now accept that the mind and the brain are separate aspects of our nature. This was revolutionizing psychology and even impacting medicine, leading to entirely new methods of teaching while leaving much rote learning behind. Lucia clarified how the overlapping of education and psychology revealed the synthesis and interdependence of both. She has mentored many other thought leaders in both fields. It was said she has an exceptional presence, a heart of gold, and a mind on fire. Lucia's speeches were incredibly inspiring. She was glorified not just as an educator, but also as a wise woman and superb human being. How many people recognized or wondered about her true stature?

Rexi Buntaran is a scientific genius from Jakarta, Indonesia, who excels in different fields. He developed a process to separate the hydrogen and oxygen atoms of water safely and efficiently, producing high levels of energy which could be captured and used. Rexi then invented an automobile engine which could run on water, getting almost a hundred miles per gallon. Rexi also apparently had just discovered a cure for two types of cancer. He was described as extraordinarily modest, ultra-calm, kind, and only slept four hours a night. He shares all his knowledge and data. Rexi had provided valuable ideas to other scientists and students, who then made their own significant breakthroughs. Many highly respected scientists said he was the smartest one—ever. Were there more than a mere handful who had guessed his true stature?

Both Rexi and Lucia were deeply humble people, focused entirely on serving the needs of others. They each had recently hinted of connections with other very special people. Do truly great leaders have any need to call themselves great?

Over the next two weeks, Theo was able to find some times to connect with Neeya via Zoom. She finished recording his intro, narrative, and closing remarks. Her videomentary editor then put the whole project together. With Zune's input, Neeya gave him a list of tweaks and, lo and behold, felt it was finally ready to go.

Neeya was paying less attention these days, but the news was getting so disturbing and hard to watch. She was trying to keep herself in the right frame of mind to produce an upbeat, inspiring documentary story. In Washington, DC, it was as if a war was taking place between Republicans and Democrats. The Middle Path party vainly tried to remain moderate and neutral, and just govern, but to no avail. The fleeting emergence of several new parties made it increasingly arduous for decisions to be made. Any new proposed legislation was at a congressional standstill. The US president was getting frequent death threats, and there were alarming rumors about the military, rogue CIA operatives, financial oligarchs, and extremist groups working with shadowy officials in Congress to oust President Prima and install someone of their own choosing. This dictatorial aristocrat would then declare martial law and let the military enforce their agenda. After all, that was what presidents were for, they thought.

Massive protests were being held in many cities over a lengthy laundry list of grave issues—out of control inflation, unemployment, a resurgence of COVID mutations killing thousands daily, severe shortages of electronic parts, frequent widespread power outages, reservoirs gone dry, and racial strife. The masses were feeling helpless. There were more violent riots between protestors and counter-protestors. Local and state elections were being disputed. The results were often too unclear to have outcomes people could accept, and many elections had more than one person claiming to have won the contested office. Life as we knew it was rapidly coming to an end. Solutions were out of reach on all the major issues. Too many people were in too much pain. The world was spinning out of control. Anxiety, frustration, and loss of hope were rampant.

Distressed by all this, Neeya found herself praying that exceptionally great leaders really would appear. *Soon. Now.* It turned out she was not the only one praying. Large prayer groups formed in many communities and cities around the world. Faith-based sermons became more focused on coping with crises and how to keep the faith. Talk of unity and harmony increased yet often lacked concrete ideas about how to make it happen. Suggestions of divine intervention were only working for some of the listeners, though many did find a shared solace in fellowship, which provided much-needed comfort.

Other people were taking matters into their own hands, hoarding food, planting rooftop and backyard gardens, or learning survival skills. Many were finding ways to be self-sufficient and get off the grid, since it was no longer reliably operating 24-7 in many areas, having long been overtaxed and unable to meet the need. Even high-efficiency heat pumps needed electricity to operate. Would there be enough gas and oil, and if there was, who could afford to keep their homes warm enough in the winter? Solar panels were still too expensive for most people and many businesses. Adults were moving back into their parents' homes to save money and share resources. Young people were a lot less likely to leave the nest after graduating high school or college.

Food banks could not keep up with demand, and food pantries were overwhelmed by middle-class people who had never been to a pantry before. Kim told Neeya she saw a sign on a suburban street in New Jersey urging "Food, Not Lawns." Grocery stores had about half their normal inventory, leaving many shelves nearly empty.

Credit card interest rates were at an amazing 34 percent, and the rate of inflation just kept rising. Mortgage rates were approaching 16 percent, leaving most people out of the housing market. Money was tight, and it had become exceedingly difficult for most folks to buy items which weren't necessary. Businesses were closing due to a lack of demand, and burglaries were becoming common. The government seemed impotent. Was the president going to resign? And if she did, what next? Neeya again feared that society as we knew it was quickly unraveling, at least in the US, where people had ignored what many countries were experiencing for decades. Europe, America, and other developed nations were being humbled in a manner never experienced before, despite having been through two World Wars.

The spreading chaos in the world motivated Neeya to get her Great Leaders videomentary out ASAP. She was tenaciously spending most of every day working on it. The last three days had been spent searching for audio clips of background music which wasn't copyrighted to avoid breaching any laws which could interfere with the project's integrity.

Corey, the videomentary editor, called Neeya with some ideas about how to get the videomentary out to the public, including one suggestion she did not like.

"Neeya, you probably know that people have really short attention spans these days. Kind of like the whole world has ADD, right? Your videomentary is half an hour, and I think that is way too long. People will lose interest in the middle, even if they like it."

Neeya was insulted. She avoided berating Corey by taking a moment to compose herself before she spoke. "So, Corey, what do you suggest?"

"Cut the length of the videomentary in half, Neeya; then more people will watch the whole thing."

"That would seriously weaken it, Corey." Her tone revealed she was still irritated.

"You spend about fifteen minutes giving background and providing material about historical leaders. My read on what you are really up to is telling us a group of Great Leaders is coming soon, but you only give that a few minutes. Cut out most of the historical stuff and put more in about them and what's coming, especially if you believe it's going to happen soon."

"I sure hope it's soon. That's what my intuition tells me, and it's why I've had those dreams." Neeya knew he was right, even though it bothered her to have to cut out weeks and weeks of hard, good work.

"What about twenty minutes, Corey?"

"Still too long, Neeya." She squirmed.

"I've always had this thing for the number eighteen, so how about eighteen minutes?" Her tone was one of surrender.

"Good decision. Let me know what to cut out, and give me a few more minutes about how you see Great Leaders emerging soon."

"It's a deal. Give me a couple of days to get back to you, Corey. Thanks so much for your wise advice, even if it bothered me so much!"

Neeya knew what she had to do, even if it was a risk. *I have to put more in about my experiences—tell people about the Prism; tell people what the energy flow will be like from the Prism, through the Muses, and out into the world; tell people that whatever goodwill is left in the world is about to get a major boost, and it can make all the difference. I think I need to have another one of those experiences. Wait a minute. That's crazy. I'm gonna sound like some weirdo false prophet. Ahhhch. I'm just a normal person who's gonna tell a story about some dreams I had. That sounds reasonable. Whew! I can do this. And I will. I want to pray, but is someone really listening?*

Over the next two days, Neeya edited the script. Theo tweaked his narrative, historical references were abbreviated, and it was sent to Corey for a final edit. He gave her a long list of sites where she could upload the videomentary to maximize exposure, including You-Tube, Facebook, Vimeo, Reddit, Instagram, and more. A great sense of relief began to replace the anxiety and frustration Neeya had been feeling, not to mention the stress of working tenaciously every day, for weeks on end.

When Corey told Neeya he was done with the edits and it was ready for her final review, she invited Zune, Amara, and Kim over to watch it with her. Her forty-two-inch, high-definition monitor was no movie theater screen, but it was just right for this purpose. Favian linked in from Senegal. Neeya was nervous that her three friends may not think it was good enough, but at this point, she was just about out of steam and hoped no further work was needed.

The four of them sat on Neeya's deep-emerald-green couch and watched the Great Leaders videomentary. When it was over, Kim exclaimed exuberantly, "Neeya! I had no idea it was going to be this good. You could win an award!" Favian was on Zoom, clapping loudly. Zune just sat there with a huge smile, silently sending Neeya his palpable approval. Amara was visibly pleased. Neeya began to softly cry tears of relief and joy. Zune held her. Kim wanted to upload it to the world right then.

Zune told Neeya, "Your script is great. The part about the Seven Muses and the Prism really comes to life. It's believable. Theo makes the whole thing work. He has such a dynamic presence—so clear, so real, so easy to like. It's obvious he is a very, very special man. I am so glad Favian was able to make the connection for you!"

"You're right, Zune. I don't know where we'd be without Theo. He sounds like a great leader too!"

"He is, Neeya," responded Zune with deep sincerity.

Neeya imagined the Muses and the Prism were looking over her shoulder right now, satisfied with the videomentary, ready to be invited into public view. Then humanity will realize our innate unity, galvanizing the spread of goodwill to make real changes possible.

Neeya earnestly shared her thought aloud: "Humanity is at a crossroads now. I hope we choose the right path ahead."

Neeya had no idea how dramatically her life was about to change again. The videomentary was going viral. She was thrilled and proud of her work. During the next few weeks, Neeya was inundated with calls and emails. People she hardly knew or used to know were getting in touch.

Neeya fervently hoped a growing expectation that Great Leaders really were coming to help out would somehow evoke their arrival. It would have seemed totally crazy a couple of months ago, but now, she was fired up by her dream experiences.

Those experiences, the Muses and the Prism...I can feel their energy. It's still with me. Can't it be with anyone? I don't know how, but if all this is real, then everyone should be able to feel it. But how can those exquisite vibes be spread? I have no idea how. Guess it's up to them. Seems my part is done.

When Theo called to express his delight about the videomentary, Neeya found herself with tears again. It was a healthy kind of crying, even though she was embarrassed. Theo explained to her how the assistant secretary general of the UN was outraged to learn Theo had gone through with the project and decided to have him suspended and demoted. It would undermine his career. However, the next day, the UN secretary general called him to say he was overriding Theo's boss, as he was okay with the videomentary, and Theo would be retaining his position. Neeya quickly moved from angst to relief. She was gushing with gratitude and praise for Theo's role. And Theo was deeply grateful Neeya had come up with the idea and included him. They both felt useful.

Accolades were all over social media. Most of it was for Theo, who had become the star of the show. Neeya got plenty of recognition too, but Theo was the face of it and the focus of attention. It was not all roses though. While most of the response was highly positive, much was sharply negative.

Many religious people, especially Christians, were highly offended. The videomentary was at odds with beliefs about the Rapture, or Armageddon. Many Shia Muslims were upset, since their belief included how the Imam Mahdi would appear by himself in Mecca. Many Hindus also became disturbed, as they did not expect Krishna to return until far in the future. Numerous Buddhists were not on board with the prophecy either, given their expectation that the next Buddha would not arrive for thousands of years. *Oh well. This isn't prophecy. I just made up a story about my dreams. I just want to inspire and give people hope.*

CHAPTER 11

As Neeya was leaving her apartment that afternoon, she saw a group of about twenty people angrily protesting in front of her building. She wondered what was happening and was stunned to see it was about her. The signs and the harsh chanting accused her of blasphemy. Her *Great Leaders* videomentary went against the Bible, they said. Before they could recognize her, she pulled her hoodie up over her head and hurried away as quickly as possible.

Oh my God! This is insane. I only told a story about a possibility. I am not against anything. Can't we all have our own beliefs? I'm not angry at them for what they believe. How on earth am I going to live with this, with angry people stomping around, yelling right at my front door?

When Neeya came back a few hours later, still scared, she surveyed the scene from a block away to find the crowd was gone. Up went the hoodie again as she quickly ducked inside the building.

What if they get physical? I can't stay here. I gotta find a safe place till this blows over. Forget Angela; she may let those nasty people inside. Zune is staying with a friend and doesn't have his own place. Favian is across the ocean. I'll ask Kim. She's always supportive, and I trust her. Kim responded, "Of course you can, Neeya." Neeya thanked her effusively. She would organize herself, pack up, and head over to Kim's after dark.

I was naive to imagine only good responses to the videomentary. Given the state of the world today, it makes sense that for every person who loves the Great Leaders idea, there would be one person who hates it. Why can't we disagree with each other without the hate? Can't we just agree to accept our differences? What's that phrase…? Oh yeah—disagree better. That's a cool way to go.

Neeya was getting contacted by the media, some mainstream and some fringe, asking for interviews. She was overwhelmed, uncertain, and wanting to retreat and hide. Neeya called Zune that evening, gladly taking him up on his offer to screen contacts from the media, being highly selective in approving just a couple of interviews for Neeya.

"Zune, I would be lost without you."

"Neeya, it must be that destiny thing. I had no idea what would happen when I took this detour from my Journey on the Infinite Highway. I guess this isn't a detour. Feels like a main attraction."

"Thank goodness for that detour, Mr. Zune!"

However, it was Theo who was still getting most of the attention. He was granted permission by the UN to give several interviews. These were widely distributed by the media, and in a matter of a few weeks, Theo quickly became a familiar face around the world, as the *Great Leaders* videomentary continued to trend widely.

"Zune, sometimes I think maybe I'm crazy to believe in all this Great Leaders stuff. I mean, it can feel way too over-the-top wonderful, but then I remember my dreams and the talk with Emmanuel, and in my heart, I know it's true."

"Extraordinarily great leaders really are coming. Thanks to you, Neeya, many millions now expect them. This will help humanity be receptive to their presence and their work. They will not announce themselves as leaders. They will simply and totally excel in their own fields of activity. They will inspire and point the way. Humanity will do the work."

"I hope you're right, Zune," was Neeya's humble response. "But will people know they really are, well, great?"

"Yes, they will. These Great Souls have the highest level of integrity and character. They have no wrong inclinations or bad habits. And it won't just be about them. They will support and work through individuals and groups who do good work—those who are seen as experts in their own fields. These Great Souls have a loving and dynamic presence which will easily make them unique."

"Can you say a little more about them, Zune?"

"These men and women who are the Great Ones will be examples of selfless service. They will encourage right attitudes toward material living."

"Zune, what about the one I call the Prism?"

"He is *the* Great One."

"Is he coming too?"

"Yes. I refer to him as the Coming One." Neeya got the chills.

"These Great Leaders have begun to speak openly about the emergence of the one you call the Prism. Due to the extraordinarily high level of respect they have, not only from their coworkers but from so many highly renowned people, a climate of hope and expectancy has begun to spread around the world for such an appearance. You have begun to see this already. Celebrities, politicians, business executives, and people in academia, as well as religious leaders, are now openly expecting them now.

"What an incredible development, Zune!"

"The Prism focalizes and potentizes the united efforts of the Great Leaders. He works to mediate fear, conflict, and chaos in the world. The spread of goodwill is one of the key methods to do so. These Great Souls fulfill their part in a coordinated and constantly evolving plan to support humanity. I try to grasp what tiny role I can play in what some call the Plan. Then I make an effort to materialize it. Of course, it can be a serious challenge to truly know what my part is and then to accomplish it. It frequently varies. Even so, I must give it my best, maintaining intention no matter what."

"I am hearing this has become a hot topic at many religious gatherings," Neeya responded. "Some believe what you are describing will happen, while others don't, since it doesn't correspond to their expectations of such a—what do you call it?—an emergence, I guess. Seems it's a good conversation to have either way. And there's starting to be tons of stuff about this on social media too."

"True, Neeya. Personally, I do think something spectacular is on the imminent horizon."

Intuitively, Neeya responded inwardly to Zune's words, bolstering her conviction the dreams are a hint of what is about to manifest. They were both quiet for a moment, trying to digest this grand vision of a profound possibility.

Neeya and Zune both sensed that the world was rapidly approaching a dramatic quantum point. *It's frightening. Humanity may have to walk across hot coals to reach the other side. Then, everything can finally start to get better. The Great Leaders sure are coming just in time.*

Neeya was easily comfortable at Kim's apartment and felt safe there. She and Zune were having email, phone, and Zoom contact multiple times a day. With Kim's okay, they decided it would be easier for now if Zune also stayed there, even if it meant he'd be sleeping on the couch in the living room. When Kim told him he was a role model of being adaptable, Zune was too humble to agree, only saying softly, "Glad to help, Kim."

Neeya decided to take an updated look at what was happening on social media in response to her project. She came across plenty of pros and cons, but what really caught her attention was that she was not the only one having 'special' dreams. She read some postings from others, and while the details varied greatly and none were exactly just like hers, what they had in common was the expectation that someone is coming—someone special. A few had dreams about an emerging group of Great Souls. Many of the postings seemed over-the-top weird and fanatical. Neeya hoped they wouldn't detract from her own story.

It was still rather strange for Neeya to find herself thinking about this Great Leaders theme at all. It was not on her radar before the vivid dreams. She couldn't prove there really were such people yet knew she had to tell the story. *And that's what it is: just my story.*

Neeya sat at the desk in Kim's spare bedroom gazing out at massive, cottony clouds cruising silently in the blueness beyond. She was deeply pondering—some would call it meditating on—her dreams. Neeya wondered if she could have presented a more generic version which may not have antagonized so many people. She quickly let go of the thought, realizing she had been true to herself. Neeya told her story just as she had experienced it. *Sure, it all could be imaginary stuff coming from my own subconscious, but in my heart, I will always believe it's real and that it's right to act on it. This must be why I have felt so different lately. Despite the stress and all the negativity coming my way, I still feel the energy flowing from the Prism, through the Muses, out into the world. It's good energy, good for my soul. And that's what it's all about! Do what you want with it, folks!*

That's how Neeya explained it when she was interviewed. "I'm just a regular person. I had some inner experiences that blew me away, and I'm sharing them with you, just in case you find it possible or helpful. And don't believe me just because I said it. If it sounds good to you, then in your own way, check it out. Trust your intuition. See if you can prove it's true—or false. Ultimately, you should only accept something like this if you can verify it through your own experience." During her interviews, she always praised Theo, trying to draw attention away from herself. "This is not about me. Ignore me. Just check out the *Great Leaders* videomentary and do what you want with it." Her integrity was appreciated by many, who may have otherwise seen her as a deluded dreamer.

As Theo suddenly became highly popular on social media, he also gave interviews, making a real effort to shy away from stating anything sounding like a religious prophecy. The need for true leaders was generally acknowledged, especially at the UN. As long as he kept a generic focus on leaders and leadership, he was good to go. Given his down-home yet sophisticated, erudite manner of speaking, plus his magnetic charm, most people loved listening to him.

Theo's interviews were now seen on TV as well as social media, and some viewers began to see him as a Great Leader. He humbly denied this, describing himself as a humanitarian instead. Very soon, he was in great demand. This was unexpected. Theo's time was limited though. Zune and Neeya were overjoyed to see such a positive note being sounded, even if there was an intense backlash by those who felt Theo was a threat undermining their staunch religious beliefs.

The UN Economic and Social Council was about to hold a high-level international forum on multiple current crises, and the secretary general suggested Theo could give a major speech. It would be televised, and millions around the globe would see it. Until recently, these forums were barely noticed, but now that the public was fascinated with Theo, people all over would be watching. It was conceived as an opportunity to promote leadership development and how it would be good for the UN as well. Most importantly, Theo felt it could help generate enough goodwill to take some of the wind out of the negativity now so rampant throughout the world. He was surprised yet honored, agreeing to give the talk just ten days from now. Neeya's videomentary had sparked something truly special.

It was an incredibly hectic, intense time for Neeya. She asked Zune to go outside for a walk with her, hoping it would be relaxing and gently reinvigorating. "I need to get some fresh air," she told him. "I need to breathe and de-stress."

"Sure, Neeya. I'll go with you. Anytime."

I wish you would *go with me anytime—every time.* She wanted to say this out loud, but things were going so wonderfully well with Zune alongside her being incredibly supportive, Neeya didn't want to risk rocking the boat. *How can a man be so together, so steady, so present? Okay, yeah, I admit it: I love him. But if I tell him, it may ruin things.*

Neeya hesitantly opened the door to the street, worried protestors may have found her "safe house" with Kim, only to behold a major disturbance outside. She instinctively moved behind Zune, gripping his upper arms tightly, seeking safety. He felt her rapid breath, hot and moist, on the nape of his neck. He stood strong and still. With Zune before her, Neeya felt protected.

The scene was not what she anticipated. People were moving in various directions, agitated, gesturing, looking at their cell phones, shouting unintelligibly. Neeya and Zune just stood there taking it all in, slowly making sense of what was happening. They had spent the morning relaxing, having agreed not to pick up their phones or turn on their laptops or the TV. It was a rare few hours of being off the media grid. They were missing the biggest story in many years.

Neeya and Zune hastily retreated upstairs, back into Kim's apartment. Zune turned on the TV, scrolling through several news stations. Neeya did the same on her laptop. It quickly became clear. There was an attempted coup of the United States government in progress. It was a domestic terrorist attack aimed at removing President Leeanne Prima, installing someone else, and taking control of Congress and major governmental departments, including the military.

Zune and Neeya were shocked. The rumors they'd heard weeks ago had turned out to be true. They quickly found a statement online published by the insurrectionists. They had to intervene, they stated—"Russia is threatening to invade NATO nations in Europe which had aided Ukraine. China has surrounded Taiwan. India and Pakistan are at the brink of another war, exchanging threats of tactical nuclear attacks. Iran is threatening to nuke Israel. The global economy is a house of cards which is collapsing. Even the US is experiencing food shortages." Their biggest concern was accusations that "President Prima is in over her head, doing nothing, and it is necessary to intervene so we can replace her." However, there was no mention of who or what that could be.

Hundreds of thousands of people began streaming into Washington, DC, to protect the president and the democracy. Others were moving to support the attempted coup. It was not clear exactly who was in charge of the coup or just what the current status of things was. It was evident that radical extremists and militias were moving toward government buildings and President Prima was out of sight.

"Has she been captured?" Neeya anxiously asked. "How can this be happening in America?" she wondered aloud, her voice quivering. "And I thought it was about me! How naive."

Suddenly, most stations flashed the face of President Prima on the screen. She was making a statement. "I am in a safe, undisclosed location. The vice president is at another safe location. We absolutely are still in office. We will remain in office. Despite the claims of the domestic terrorists, Congress has not been impacted, and it will not be. Our government and our democracy continue to function."

Neeya and Zune listened in hushed silence. They opened Kim's fourth-floor windows to realize it had suddenly gone quiet outside.

People were listening to the president. The profound gravity of the crisis was all too obvious.

President Prima continued. "Yes, there are many legitimate concerns about the state of the world. Anarchy will never solve our problems or the many global crises we are now witnessing. This attempted insurrection can only serve to deepen our crisis, but it absolutely will not undermine our democracy which so many have given their lives to develop, protect, and sustain." She sounded very strong and very much in charge.

"The terrorists have no legal or moral right to take these actions. I have activated the National Guard, FBI, Department of Homeland Security, Secret Service, and many other law enforcement agencies. Let me be clear: this attempted coup will be stifled immediately. I am the president, and I will remain in office. I have sworn to uphold the Constitution, and I will do so. Those responsible for today's actions will be held accountable and will receive the appropriate consequences.

"Right now, I ask all of you who care about our democracy, who care about our country, to stay home, remain peaceful, and support our efforts to maintain the stability and integrity of our government. I assure you that the current situation will be resolved immediately. We will never turn into an autocratic, totalitarian state where the few can take control. In America, people have the right to speak out, to protest, to challenge the system, and to vote for whoever they want. They do not have a right to illegally and violently attempt to overthrow the government and put who they want in charge. It is *not* going to happen here, now, under my watch! This is a country of the people and by the people, not the few. I will continue to make additional announcements soon. Thank you so much for your support. God bless America. God bless everyone everywhere."

President Prima had learned the lessons of the January 6th insurrection at the US Capitol. She initiated a recently updated rapid-response plan to counter the coup attempt. The National Guard and law enforcement units were instantly on the move. The FBI and the Department of Homeland Security's Cybersecurity and Infrastructure Security department, as well as other government intelligence agencies, had been tracking electronic communications on social media and the dark web, infiltrating many extremist groups. There was widely shared knowledge that the coup attempt was being planned. They were ready for it. This was the opposite of the January 6th event, when the former president watched it unfold on TV and delayed taking action.

President Prima and a group of aides and officials among responders were in close contact. She was coordinating it all. It surely helped that she herself had been a decorated intelligence officer in the navy when she was younger.

The response plan was immediately and effectively activated. Unlike January 6, they used extensive, overwhelming force to crush the insurrection and protect democracy. Large, well-armed, rapid-response forces swiftly spread out all over Washington, DC. President Prima intended for the massive display of force to crush the insurrectionists and to disarm and arrest those breaking the law. She prayed that casualties would be limited yet was not going to let them enter federal buildings like they did at the Capitol on January 6th. Tear gas and barriers would not be enough. She vowed that she would continue to provide updates and ongoing public statements of calls for calm and stability while demonstrating her own strength and control of the situation.

She was up to the challenge. "I am the commander in chief, and I am acting accordingly!" That was just what she did.

Neeya and Zune were glued to the TV. They continually rotated between CNN, FOX, MSNBC, Google News, and PBS, seeking up-to-the-moment reporting of the evolving events in Washington. Scenes of responders skirmishing with militant insurrectionist groups trying to force their way into federal buildings, only to be powerfully repelled and arrested, were deeply disturbing yet reassuring.

Some media coverage displayed distorted fragments of zealous complaints and threats which motivated the rioters. However, it was clearly too fanatical to attract involvement from the masses, despite the vitriolic insurrectionist postings spread across the internet. The vain attempts by the insurrectionists to take control of electronic communications were rendered ineffective. Their tools were hacked and shut down by multiple government counterterrorism units or blocked by most social media outlets.

Within a few hours, it became clear that the terrible threat of a coup was ending as quickly as it started, though some turmoil in the streets lingered. President Prima continued to give hourly updates and reassurances of governmental stability. By sundown she was broadcasting these from the White House, now surrounded and protected by tens of thousands of heavily armed police and National Guard troops with hundreds of large, armored vehicles. A dusk-to-dawn curfew within twenty miles of Washington, DC, was established. The president made it clear the curfew would be lifted soon if the coup threat completely ended and things calmed down.

"Zune, I can't believe this is happening in America!"

"Unfortunately, Neeya, given how polarized it has become, and how much distrust, hatred, and misinformation there is here, it was bound to happen."

"Maybe so, but the intense level of hate and the willingness to use violence scares the heck out of me. I still feel nauseous."

"That's certainly understandable. It may be too easy to say this, but considering what we just saw over the last few hours, if we let those people make us afraid and doubt what we know to be true, then they are doing their job: creating terror and undermining the rule of law. Sure, things need to seriously change, but violence is not the way. We need to be able to work through differences, no matter how strong, and discover ways we can agree to disagree without the violence. That's true whether it is between two people, two political groups, or two countries."

"You're right, Zune. Humanity has to grow up. We've been around for who knows how many millions of years. It's time to figure out how to make compromises, cooperate, and find common areas of agreement, even if it's only enough to stabilize things and maybe create a shared baseline."

"Absolutely. If we can't do it, things will only get worse, and who knows where that will lead? If we can do this, then our world can be a healthier, more harmonious place, and I don't mean some la-la-land utopia. I'm talking about people just finding ways to get along with each other despite their differences.

"Hey, Neeya. Can you imagine folks from an advanced galaxy checking out our planet, observing all the wars, poverty, materiality, greed, and pollution, not to mention silly TV commercials? They would think we were still primitives living in the stone age. Walking on the moon, understanding DNA, and having the internet doesn't make us advanced. Having a society where we recognize and work for the common good and have figured out how to live together despite our differences…maybe these are the virtues of an advanced society, the virtues of a planet which will not destroy itself but will prosper."

"Zune, I should have put that in the *Great Leaders* videomentary."

"Maybe you can do that in the next one, Neeya."

"I was hoping one would be enough." Neeya chuckled.

"You never know what's coming, partner."

It was well after midnight before Neeya and Zune felt the situation in Washington had stabilized enough so they could stop watching the news. Exhausted yet relieved, they again fell asleep together on the couch in a tender, patonic embrace.

12 CHAPTER

In the few days leading up to Theo's speech at the UN, the turbulence in America intensified even more so. Many felt like the country was becoming a banana republic. The attempted coup led to the presence of law enforcement and National Guard troops in front of municipal, county, state, and federal buildings. Some felt safer, while others felt more threatened. Raucous quarrels were common in stores, on the streets, and even between parents at their kids' soccer games. The Democrats and Republicans in Congress remained at each other's throats. The Middle Path party was not generating the level of interest and support expected. Large corporations and high-end donors were accused of usurping power from and manipulating members of Congress. Many major companies were now facing boycotts.

European and Asian governments were also seeing an alarming increase in instability. Africa continued to experience much turmoil. Citizens didn't want to await elections in order to accomplish regime changes. Hundreds of thousands were out in the streets in many cities, opposing the status quo or working to sustain and protect it. The atmosphere around the globe had become charged to the nth degree with tension. Polarization and partisanship were exceedingly rampant.

While all this was happening, the planet itself seemed to join in the mayhem. After decades of drought in the southwestern US caused thousands of arid farms to dry up, the record-setting snowstorms of the last winter, coupled with frequent torrential rainstorms and atmospheric rivers, had now resulted in severe flooding and landslides. The central valley in California was under nearly two feet of water, causing an almost complete loss of the harvest which had reliably reaped so much of America's produce for so long.

Media outlets were covering breaking news regarding the massive ice sheet which had broken off Greenland. This stupendous hunk of ice covered 12,000 square miles. Coastal cities along the Atlantic and Pacific Oceans were facing imminent risk in the next few weeks due to rising sea levels, potentially causing apocalyptic flooding. News commentators and experts wondered aloud how this and other climate disasters, like rampant wildfires covering much of Europe and North America in smoke, could be effectively managed by populations full of distrust. One pundit exclaimed, "If we don't realize every one of us has this climate disaster in common, and we do have to solve it in common, then how on earth are we going to be able to prevent ending up with a planet essentially unlivable for human beings? And I am talking about next year, not next century!"

Climate crises were emerging dramatically on vaster scales. Most citizens were unable to grasp the magnitude of it, mindlessly settling into an avoidant complacency. Another commentator questioned the audience: "It is way too late for denial. If you are in the mountains and see an avalanche starting in the snowy peaks above, do you just stand there, hoping it will stop or bypass you, or do you take protective action ASAP?"

Later that night Neeya had another one of those vivid, profound dreams. It was different this time. Instead of the Muses and the Prism sitting in an ethereal room, they were each in separate locations around the world. The Muses shared an energetic force field Neeya could feel. It was as if their minds and hearts had invisible threads of living, flowing energy, some connecting with Neeya. Every thread had its own purpose, used by each Muse for projects they were coordinating. She couldn't understand how it worked, but it was an energetic grid, in existence for eons—a benevolent, useful, etheric grid. Despite being physically far apart, the Muses were transmitting the energy out into the world in a harmonious synthesis. *Are they telepathic?* The vibe of it all touched her soul deeply and exquisitely, remaining alive within her.

Neeya awoke knowing she had again been gifted with the experience of an existing reality, though most of humanity was oblivious to it. Neeya always felt that almost all of the material out there about enlightened masters, teachers from the inner dimensions, or New Age channeling was utter fantasy, to put it nicely. Now she knew that a very minimal fraction of those fantasies was actually based on a reality rarely glimpsed.

The main takeaway Neeya had was how the Muses had begun to emerge into the world, becoming recognized for their work with people. *Some of them have become known to us, even if we don't recognize them for who they truly are, yet. Could the Prism possibly be someone we'll recognize? Hard to believe, but maybe...*

Neeya was now absolutely convinced the dream experiences were real events. *Guess I need a new definition of what "real" means. Are "real" things only what I can experience with my five senses? UV rays are real. They burn my skin in the summer sun, but I can't perceive them. This stuff is way too complicated for me. Who really knows how all this works? Emmanuel? Zune?*

Neeya recalled the "order" Emmanuel had mentioned, which Amara and Zune seemed to know about. Then she realized—*the Muses are the true Great Leaders humanity needs. But how can they lead if no one can see them?* She could not believe any kind of energy flow could be enough to make a global difference, even though it sure was more than enough for her. *We need to see these Great Souls in the flesh! At least, I do. I have no idea how in the world this is gonna happen, but it will be incredibly cool when it does!*

Neeya couldn't wait to tell Zune about her latest dream. "So I just gotta ask, again: Do you think something like this is actually going to play out in public view, Zune?"

"To be honest, I do. You have witnessed it because you have a role to play."

"That sounds crazy, Zune."

"Maybe so, Neeya. When we hear about people supposedly having contact with groups like the Masters of Wisdom or a planetary network of advanced beings, I think that, almost always, they are merely in contact with their own subconscious or maybe even the subconscious of others.

"I do like the term spiritual hierarchy, Neeya, but it is not what you think. It has nothing to do with authority. It's about levels of consciousness. Ignoring anything esoteric, you can easily look around and see that people have various levels of consciousness. Some are only focused on whatever is immediately before them on the most material, concrete levels. Others are capable of more abstract creative thinking. And some are able to be aware of almost everything around them and can understand the cause and meaning of whatever they encounter. Some are selfish, while others have a heart of gold that warms the heart of others.

"If you do want to get esoteric, Neeya, a very rare few are conscious on more subtle levels, aware of things outside of our five senses. And if you want to include the mind as the sixth sense, their conscious experience even goes well beyond that into deep realms of intuition."

Neeya told him of a line she recalled from a song way back in the sixties by the Incredible String Band: "I found a door behind my mind, and that's the greatest treasure."

"Well, I'd sure like to find that door, Zune. And then go through it."

Zune smiled, continuing: "There are levels of consciousness available to all of us but nearly impossible to attain, since we limit ourselves to a focus on our bodily experience of the physical world via our five senses. There is more to the universe than that. And there have always been more, well, evolved people who live in the here and now as well as on the more subtle inner levels too. I think the core group of Great Leaders—or should we just call them Great Souls?—has a consciousness that is realms beyond what most of us experience. And ultimately, we are all connected in the realms of the soul."

"That sure is a lot to take in, Zune!"

"Absolutely."

"And how many people do you think expect them or hope they will appear?"

"A real lot of people do. All the major religions have prophecies related to this. Since your videomentary has gone totally viral, millions are now thinking about them, and so many are expecting them. Perhaps this will help invoke them, making it easier for them to externalize."

"Maybe, Zune, but it all sounds so crazy!"

He simply smiled for a long time. Neeya thought, *It's like he knows how it all works.* She sat there with him in one of their silent interludes, trying to take it all in, asking herself, *Why me?*

"It doesn't matter why you, Neeya." *Did he just hear what I was thinking?*

"Just accept that it is happening, and if your intuition tells you it's real, then please keep going with it. After all, so far so good! And hopefully Theo's speech at the UN will give the Great Muses a great intro!"

"Zune, are *you* my muse?" Neeya asked, sincerely curious yet half joking.

"Maybe your own soul is your muse, Nee." She quivered inside herself.

A silent interlude followed. *So much to take in. So much to process and understand. I have to ask him more about this real soon.*

Neeya and Zune were given special passes to hear Theo's speech in a large conference room at the UN, as the public was no longer allowed to attend events in the general assembly due to security concerns. The UN was facing its own challenging crossroads. Denigrated by many as weak and ineffective, others saw it as the hope of the world and the only practical, realistic way to meaningfully address issues of a global nature.

Neeya arrived first, in awe of the great variation in human diversity she beheld. The room was comfortably crowded with people of just about every color, attired in various styles of dress. She heard languages being spoken which she could not identify. Neeya was intrigued that despite their outer differences, the people in the room seemed eager to hear Theo deliver his talk. After all, she knew that was what folks needed right now if things were going to get better. So many feared it wouldn't. Climate disasters were an obvious existential threat, but if the world's economies continued to implode, civilization as we knew it could go through an uncomfortable dismantling. At least, this would be true in the developed nations. Countries in the early stages of development, or even just emerging, had a lot less to lose as they did not have much economic or commercial infrastructure yet. *It's definitely time for some good news.*

Moments before the speech was about to commence, Zune arrived. Neeya noticed he appeared slightly flushed, an evident trace of concern in his face.

"Zune, are you okay?"

"Now I am," he replied, speaking very softly.

"What's the matter?"

"I was visiting a diplomat I know from a member nation in South America. I had just left her office and ended up in the same administrative wing where Theo was. Just as he entered the hallway, maybe twenty feet from me, I saw a man run toward him with his arm raised, holding something in his hand."

"Oh my God, Zune! Then what?"

"I yelled out, 'Theo!' I only had time to shout his name. He turned as the man lunged at him with a knife. Theo flung his right forearm out just in time to hit the attacker on his wrist. The knife fell to the floor. Two security guards immediately tackled the guy and cuffed him, even though he was seriously struggling. Theo and other high-level diplomats were quickly ushered to another area, where they are safe."

"Oh no! Did Theo get hurt?"

"The knife never touched him. He protected himself. He may have a sore arm, but I saw the look on his face a moment afterward, and I am sure that if anyone could remain composed enough to give a speech after being attacked, it would be Theo. I think it was some kind of cosmic coincidence that I happened to end up in the same hallway at the same time and saw the man charging toward him so menacingly."

"Seems like no coincidence to me, Zune." She was freaked out but relieved.

Neeya was astonished this could happen in the UN. Zune told her it was "so sad to see, but not really all that unexpected, considering the intense level of distrust and hate all over the world.

"People can't accept differences. It's their way, or you are the enemy, and I must destroy you. It's the opposite of what the UN is all about—meeting together to figure out how to resolve our differences peacefully. We all share the same fundamental common ground. We are all part of one human family. When we can live accordingly, our world will be a much healthier place, for people and for the earth."

As the opening remarks in the general assembly began, the room became silent. No one in the audience knew what had just happened to Theo. *What a strange irony*, Neeya thought.

After a few short remarks, Theo was introduced. He began with a call to recognize our unity, even if it now seemed like a unity based mostly on sharing common crises of climate, conflict, hunger, injustice, and financial failings. Theo acknowledged the UN was often unable to adequately resolve differences, preventing it from reaching its potential effectiveness. He stated that the UN Security Council put way too much power in the hands of the five permanent members, who represented large, powerful nations.

Theo then made a startling statement, exclaiming that in this modern era, we have no need for such a council. This led to an ear-splitting symphony of cheers and jeers. Members from the smaller countries made the loudest sounds, in support of Theo's suggestion. Larger nations felt threatened they would lose much of their control. Theo was clearly putting his reputation and position on the line.

Neeya was anxious to hear him talk about Great Leaders, worried that he might not. His time was nearly up when Theo finally got there.

"Please remember that the name of the UN begins with the word *united*. Today, it is mostly a goal, just a vision"

Neeya looked around the room and could see Theo still had everyone's attention, given that he had such a unique blend of calm and dynamic charisma. *He is the ultimate nice guy that you want to have as a special friend, the kind of guy you believe simply because of who he is.*

Theo continued. "I am so very grateful to have had the honor of narrating the recent videomentary *Great Leaders* produced by my dear friend Neeya. Many of you have seen it." Neeya struggled to feel proud without letting it boost her ego.

"This is just what we need now: exceptionally great leaders." The audience murmured its agreement.

"I am going to go off script now and tell you what I really think." Theo looked around, pausing long enough to see an audience avidly awaiting his next words.

"It does not seem possible that our current crises can be solved without such special ones helping us. There truly *are* Great Souls here with us, and there always has been. Most of them are unknown to the public, functioning behind the scenes through their coworkers, whose faces we may recognize because of their good works. Great Souls are essentially as brilliant, creative, compassionate, and determined as a person can possibly be. They are our greatest human beings."

Neeya heard several people in the room mutter disapprovingly under their breath.

"Some of these Great Souls have helped birth a country, stopped a war, made dramatic discoveries, or were the inspiration starting a religion. Some have only worked from the inner side and remain unknown and unnamed. I say to you now that just like in the videomentary, there *is* a coordinated network of Great Leaders. We are already noticing some of them work openly in the world." The boos and applause from the audience grew louder.

Theo continued slowly yet forcefully. "Please understand—these Great Ones will not solve our problems. Great Leaders inspire us, point out the possibilities, and offer solutions. We have to do the work. All of us, each in our own way. Every contribution counts, no matter how small. All of us *can* serve the greater good." The conference room filled with applause, which did not drown out negative comments and howls from listeners who thought Theo had gone off the rails.

"Here is the real take-home message, my friends." A tactful pause resulted in the room becoming quiet again. "My forecast for you is that the Greatest One of them all will be part of the group that emerges to guide us. Just who that is, I cannot say. My fervent hope is that you will recognize him—or maybe her," Theo said with a wide grin. "Please be open to the possibility, even if it challenges what you believe or what you have been taught. Humanity is not alone. A group of our brothers and sisters who have come before us, the great saints and heroes, are still with us, ready to share the love and wisdom of the ages. And now, we are ready to respond. Keep your hearts and minds open. The spirit of peace will be shed abroad. May God bless the human race and our planet. Thank you."

The general assembly was in a raucous uproar as Theo ended his speech. There was such a din that Neeya couldn't tell the difference between those who were enraged by what Theo said and those who were inspired, willing to believe that what he said was possible.

Zune was thrilled at the unexpectedly bold comments Theo had delivered. He turned toward Neeya with a buoyant smile. Tears of joy emerged on her cheeks as Neeya stated, "I can't believe Theo just put it out there like that! Wow!" The two shared an ardent embrace.

"Neeya, it's like this speech was the perfect outcome of your vid-eomentary. Thanks to Theo, you have gotten your message across. So many people will now be receptive to a reality often disparaged as a fairy tale. My forecast is that Theo's prediction will come true."

"Oh Zune, I feel overwhelmed. Even if part of what he was bold enough to say comes true, then maybe humanity can get it together and not fall into the abyss we seem to be rapidly heading toward," Neeya exclaimed.

"That is the plan, Neeya, and we are playing our part in it."

Neeya couldn't speak. They both were anxious to get home and check out the news to find out what kind of reactions were happening in response to Theo's dramatic speech.

CHAPTER 13

Neeya and Zune sat down next to each other on the couch, eyes glued to the TV monitor. It was becoming a ritual of theirs. They waited, trying to keep a lid on their impatience. The first twenty minutes or so covered the alarming coastline sea rise of major cities due to the massive ice sheet dislocated from Greenland, the largest wildfire in California history, and how the bottom was falling out of the stock market in the US, now down 63 percent this year and still sinking.

"What about Theo's talk?" Neeya said to the TV. It sounded more like a demand than a question.

"It's coming, Neeya. Hold on."

Finally, there was some coverage of Theo's speech. Zune was disappointed it was more about the attempted assault than about the content of his message. However, it was wonderful for the two coworkers to see short clips of Theo's speech on TV, knowing many social media streams were also covering it. Zune especially appreciated that they played the last part of his speech, about the externalization of a network of Great Souls.

The coverage included the myriad emotionally charged responses now arising. Some of the loudest came from religious realms. Many were calling Theo's remarks blasphemy, as they did not correspond to their interpretation and expectation for what a so-called second coming would be like. Others accused him of becoming a religious fanatic, straying way too far from the social and environmental themes of the UN's meeting. Already, ambassadors from UN Security Council permanent nations were sounding off in vehement protest of Theo's suggestion to dismantle the council. It was no surprise they feared a reduction of their power, even while espousing themes of equity and social justice.

Neeya and Zune were thrilled to hear interviews with others who said the speech was magnificent and that it was possible that greater leaders than we have seen would soon emerge. The speech had galvanized millions who knew humanity could make changes essential to sustain itself and the health of our planet. The enthusiastic eagerness to take action and "be the change" was palpable.

"I just hope it will be in time," reflected Neeya.

"It will be, Nee."

This was another late night, absorbing all they could from the media coverage and not falling asleep until the dawn readied to reveal itself. "If the whole thing doesn't fall apart, the best is yet to come" were Zune's reassuring words.

Much attention was drawn to Neeya after her videomentary went viral. Now, after Theo's speech, she had even more requests for interviews and talks. Neeya was hesitant to move into this new role. Given Zune's encouragement to "just be yourself and talk about what really matters to you now," she began to make use of the opportunities presented to her. She stuck to the same basic theme, asking interviews to be kept short. Her message was simple: "Our world has so many profound crises, we must take them with the utmost and immediate seriousness. Truly great leaders are arriving and can help, but it's up to all of us to play our little parts as best we can."

Despite the efforts of the media to lure her into addressing what some called spiritual prophecies, she was mostly able to avoid discussing anything overtly religious or philosophical. "I'm just a regular person who crafted a story based on a series of vivid dreams. I am not an expert on anything. These are not prophecies, just a possibility I imagine will happen soon." Her humble, nonauthoritative approach made it easier for many to be receptive. Neeya did not brag or call attention to herself, coming across as just a regular person. Of course, it helped that she was pretty with a gentle, vibrant way about her. Theo was believable for another reason. His magnetic, powerful presence gave his words such strong impact.

Zune and Neeya sat on the couch, chatting over their morning coffee.

"I am so incredibly grateful that you are here to support me in all this, Zune."

"Now I understand why I took this particular detour from the Infinite Highway, Neeya—to run into you and help you with what you've done." Neeya wondered what he really meant, even if their meeting each other was "meant to be." *How does that kind of thing actually work? Did Zune plan it? Does he know more than he's letting on?*

"I hope you will keep helping me with what I am doing. It often feels overwhelming."

"Well, Neeya, this has been pretty much perfect, yet it's getting time for me to move onward again. My Journey must continue. Always."

"I'm not sure exactly what your Journey is, Zune. How do you know when you get to what you call your destination?"

"My intuition whispers a hint to follow a certain exit sign, so I take it. Each stop on the way is a destination unto itself. Here, in this city with you, I have been at the right destination—a most special one." Neeya got goose bumps hearing him affirm this.

"Actually, Neeya, this Journey never really ends. That's why I call it the Infinite Highway of Life."

"Who are you, really, Zune?" she asked with earnest inquisitiveness.

"Sometimes I imagine I am what I call 'everyman.' If you took all the people on the planet and mixed them together and it came out as one person, one human being who had all the challenges and all potentials within himself, maybe that's who I am."

Neeya spoke slowly. "I get it now. You can't tell me who you really are. I have to figure it out for myself." He nodded, ever so slightly. "Every day I come to see you more and more as so special, so unique, Zune."

"Special, no. Unique, maybe."

"But you totally understood all I was doing with the Great Leaders stuff. You were already familiar." She paused, trying to get up the courage to ask him, directly. "Okay, so please tell me Zune, do you, uh, work with Great Leaders?" Asking this aloud caused Neeya to feel uneasy. Curiosity had gotten the best of her.

Zune looked right into her eyes, deeply, softly saying "I try to" and then quickly looked away. Neeya read it as the end of the conversation. He had shared all he wanted to, giving her hints he would not expand upon. *That's enough for me to digest for now.*

They sat quietly together again, these moments often so much more valuable than dialogue. It is wise to leave space without words. Thoughts settle and coalesce. Information becomes understanding. Knowledge becomes wisdom.

Their vibes meshed. They understood themselves, each other, and the meaning they gleaned from all that was happening—no need to talk. They could just be present in the moment.

Outside her window a pigeon perched on the railing, its iridescent purple hues catching her eye. She found joy in the beautiful colors rippling with each of the pigeon's rapid breaths. Neeya was taken in by its piercing eyes, swiftly surveying the world in all directions, body poised and ready. In a surging splash of wings, it rose aloft beyond her building, quickly gaining altitude only to coast and then soar off into the blue. The bird transcended its earthly base, rising into the heavens.

Neeya understood that Zune was approaching the time to leave town, and she wanted to get his help in figuring out what to do next.

Zune came over the next day and made Neeya a cup of Darjeeling black tea with just a bit of maple syrup to sweeten it—her favorite. She began to miss him, even though he was still here. A tear emerged. He leaned over and kissed it away. Neeya felt the love. A soft, sweet sorrow arose. She tried to let it go.

"What are you going to do next with your life, Neeya?"

She chuckled sheepishly. "I was hoping you had an idea about how I can proceed from here, Zune."

"My idea is to help you figure that out for yourself." She loved his smile.

"Well, I want to be done with interviews and requests for another videomentary. I want to be working with people, not sitting at a desk in front of a computer."

"Makes sense, Neeya. You are so likeable, and you have a great way with people."

"Thanks." She blushed.

"How about this: What do you think are the most important things for people to know and act on now to really make a difference in the world? Please keep it practical."

"Okay, so I'll skip something kinda corny, like just loving one another. Besides, somebody said that two thousand years ago, and it sure hasn't been fully embraced yet." Neeya found her heart troubled by her own words.

"What else, Neeya? What theme do folks really need to embrace?"

"The primary need is to be truly concerned with the common good. If we did, our world would be in such a better state."

Zune nodded. She could tell he was waiting for more. It came to her right away, yet she paused for a moment to make sure it was her intuition, not just a random thought popping into her head.

Zune prompted her by asking, "What is needed so that people are motivated to work for the common good? What ingredient would your recipe need?"

Neeya paused again. "Goodwill. Yes, goodwill. Most of us aren't quite ready to love one another, but we *can* spread goodwill." Neeya became excited. "That can make all the difference!"

"Sounds spot on to me. So tell me how you can do something with this idea, how you can work on it with other people."

"I don't know right this second, but I think it's what I have to do. I hope I don't have to start some kind of organization, a nonprofit or whatever. With the money I've been getting for the interviews, I probably have enough to seed some kind of little nonprofit start-up. But I have no idea who could work on it with me. It's gotta be a group thing, not me alone."

Zune smiled and nodded. Neeya knew he approved. Another pause.

"That's what I am going to do. I have no idea how, but I will find a way."

"If it is truly the right thing for you to do, Neeya, you will find a way. And the right people will show up at the right time, just like I showed up for you."

Neeya hugged him as hard as she could. *He says the most profound things so simply!*

Neeya spent several days trying to come up with an idea for her next step. She didn't like the challenge at first but wanted to get a message out, one that was more practical than "We need Great Leaders, and they are coming." Neeya kept wondering about a vivid catchphrase encapsulating the theme, something galvanizing which could be widely embraced. *After all, society is sure unlikely to undergo some kind of major*

transformation in the immediate future unless it is forced to—for the wrong reasons. But hey, inspiration from Great Leaders might do it!

Gotta be careful. If people think Great Leaders are going to come and solve everything, they may keep sitting on their hands waiting for leaders to fix it all, and that's not gonna happen.

Feeling stuck, Neeya gave a call to her new friend Amara, hoping she had an idea which would be helpful. After the hellos and how are yous, Neeya got right down to business.

"Amara, I have to start some kind of group to take things further—for people who are open to seeing things in a new way, who care about each other and all of us but don't yet have meaningful ways to do something about it. Maybe we need a simple place to go, online, to get deeper ideas and be able to connect with others who already are having similar thoughts."

"That sounds good. What do you have in mind, Neeya?"

"That's the problem, Amara. I have all kinds of ideas swirling around inside my mind. Can't quite get a focus going."

"Well, what is the take-home message here? What is the message you want to get across now?"

"I'm concerned people may miss the point. Great Leaders are not going to take care of our problems themselves. They will offer ideas and insight. People who are already in leadership roles in their own fields will probably respond, as well as the many people working with them. The energy, ideas, and guidance trickles down. We, the people, still have to do the work!"

Neeya continued, "The most I can hope for is that we begin to think differently—about each other and about the world. I guess it can be based on what we have in common. Yep, the common good!

Wow, if we all truly care about the common good and live accordingly, it will result in some serious changes. That gets back to goodwill and having the Christmas spirit every day. Isn't this possible? It better be, or this planet is in more trouble than I want to imagine."

"Just do it, Neeya. You can if your heart is truly in it."

"My soul feels fired up. I know others are doing similar work. Maybe I'll find a new way to move beyond slogans and inspire people to take practical, concrete action."

"Neeya, let go of that 'maybe' stuff. If your soul is really fired up, you will do it, and you will succeed."

"Those are nice words, Amara, yet very humbling. It feels like something is changing inside me. My spirit is growing, driving me onward."

"Just get off the phone with me, then, and get to work, Neeya. Just do it."

"You remind me of Zune. I love you, Amara!"

From paralegal to videomentary producer to organizer for the common good, all in less than one year. Who, me? Life has so much momentum now. Gotta ride this wave, wherever it's taking me. Gotta go with the current and stay there.

Neeya did just that. Over the next few weeks, she found herself engrossed in connecting with others who shared concerns for the common good. There was another large group of people who wanted to connect with her about Great Leaders, yet Neeya thought maybe her work with that was done. She had distributed the videomentary; Theo had dramatically made the message clear. *I don't know what else I can do about it right now.*

Neeya continued to feel the vibes coming from the Prism and through the group of Muses. She found it hard to describe to others.

It felt warm and uplifting. *Nowadays, it's with me all the time. It gives me a sense of the sacred.* Though she still shied away from trying to define what sacred meant. *It has something to do with a profound reverence for others and all life, but I don't want to sound like a preacher or some fake guru.*

Neeya sought simple, everyday language, keeping the focus on what the average person can do for the common good. She elucidated, "As Great Leaders really do emerge, people will have the opportunity to respond. Then we can take small steps, ultimately resulting in big changes. I will just do what I can here locally, hooking up with others who see that if we embrace our commonality, we will be working to help get our world back on track."

The Dalai Lama said, "My religion is kindness." And Ziggy Marley has that song called "Love Is My Religion." Makes it sound so easy, huh? But it's not—at least not for me. Kindness, yes. Love, well, I'm working on that one.

Searching around the internet, Neeya found there were many groups and organizations working on themes about the common good and unity. She just wanted to connect with others locally and see where it might go. *Okay, maybe, just maybe, we can talk about Great Souls, but this gig needs to be practical. Gotta stay grounded, like the "Think globally, act locally" slogan.*

At the first meeting to start planning an initiative promoting the common good, Neeya was very clear with her new coworkers. "The way I see it, my role was just to put it out there. People can think and do what they want. I certainly did not expect such strong reactions, but it is what it is, and that's okay. After all, we can't go much further downhill if we are still going to have a decent world left in the coming decades."

Neeya's videomentary proved to be seriously stimulating in various ways. Numerous people stepped forward, declaring things like "I am the Messiah" or "So-and-so is Jesus come back" or accusing Neeya of being a false prophet. It caused much turmoil and even antagonism in religious circles. Zune told Neeya, "At least people are talking about the Great Ones, and millions are now brave enough to expect them to appear. Sermons in churches, temples, and mosques are now featuring themes addressing this, leaving many people either inspired or confused by it all."

A multitude of people around the globe, living in both rural and urban areas or merely entirely off the grid, were completely oblivious to Neeya's videomentary. Another billion or so were offended. These were primarily Muslims, Jews, Christians, Buddhists, and Hindus, who had contrary beliefs about a Coming One. They dismissed Neeya's message as false, or worse. Atheists felt it was a vaporous, religious meme or a worthless, deluded fantasy.

Some interpreted events in the world as the beginning of Armageddon, expecting the end of the world. Others passively awaited the Rapture, impotent inertia preventing them from taking effective action.

Yet hundreds of millions were inspired in a positive way by the videomentary. Their hope and expectancy for an arrival of Great Ones was growing every day, even if previously thought of as only a vague possibility or something entirely off their radar. Many were sure it would happen in their lifetime.

Millions prayed, hoping to invoke the emergence of the Greatest One. Others, believing the feminine principle in the universe was strengthening, expected the Greatest One to be a woman this time.

When Neeya was asked the standard question, "What about Jesus?" she responded by saying, "I don't know, but what do you think he would be talking about if he showed up tomorrow?" Sometimes she shared Zune's fictional comedic skit about an average guy named Mateo Melendez who meets Jesus on a New York City street:

Mateo. Yo, dude, is that really you? Like, the real Jesus?

Jesus. Yes, my son, it is I.

Mateo. This is incredible, man. What are you doing here?

Jesus. I came to offer my help. Humanity has lost its way.

Mateo. I once was lost, but like, I'm still not found, I don't think. Ha! Get it?

Jesus. Hey, don't worry; I had to fast for forty days in the burning desert to get found, but I did it. You can too.

Mateo. That's really cool, dude. Or should I say, that was really hot! So, like, are you really God's son?

Jesus. We are all children of God.

Mateo. Animals and bad people too?

Jesus. All life, brother.

Mateo. Hey, we're bros now. That's really cool.

Jesus. We sure are. We are all brothers and sisters—all of us.

Mateo. Yeah! I'm down with that. So tell me Mr. Jesus, how does the whole thing work? I mean like, God and heaven and souls and all that stuff. If anybody knows, I guess you do.

The Bible just doesn't do it for me. The ancient stories and the whole thing feels like a kid's fairy tale.

Jesus. I understand what you mean.

Mateo. Thanks. So give me an update, will ya, please? Just a short one though. I mean, like, I gotta be at work soon, okay?

Jesus. Sure. You want to know what God is? Here it is, really simple: God is all the life in the universe, in every living being—an atom, a cell, an elephant, a tree, a mountain, a planet, or even a galaxy. God is the cause of all creation and is also everything in creation.

Mateo. Gotcha, I think. Go on please.

Jesus. Life is the basic, fundamental energy pervading the entire universe.

Mateo. Is there life on other planets?

Jesus. Check this out, Mateo. There are about 100 billion galaxies. Let's say each galaxy has a billion stars. Get out your calculator, brother. Never mind, I just did the math in my head. If only one in a million stars has a planet with life—as you think of it—then maybe 10 billion planets in the universe have some kind of life. This tells us there is a lot going on out there, so don't feel lonely.

Mateo. But my girlfriend broke up with me last week.

Jesus. Stay open.

Mateo. I am open-minded.

Jesus. I meant your heart.

Mateo. Gotcha.

Jesus. Want to hear more?

Mateo. Go for it, dude. Sorry, I mean, go for it, Jesus. Hey, do you have a last name?

Jesus. Just call me Jesus. I still use that name.

Mateo. This is so cool. Yo, same question Pontius Pilate asked you back in the day: What is Truth? I mean, how does it work for a regular guy like me, huh?

Jesus. No prob, Mateo. To keep it simple, let's just say Truth is how the universe works—for human beings, anyway. If you were a planet asking me the same question, I'd have to give you a different answer.

Mateo. Thanks, but I'm just a regular guy trying to make it through each day, and it sure ain't easy, dude.

Jesus. That's why I'm here. Now, keep your mind open to my heavy riff. We are souls living in our bodies. There is a spark of true life at our very core. So the life at the core of your soul is the same energy that flows through all creation, all people. We are all connected by the same living energy. This is why we are all brothers and sisters.

Mateo. Wow, you really know what you're talking about, don't you?

Jesus. That's my job, bro.

Mateo. Yo, if I tell my ex that Jesus called me bro, you think maybe she'll get back together with me?

Jesus. Don't get distracted. Want to hear one more thing?

Mateo. Go for it.

Jesus. Remember when I said that the kingdom of heaven is within you?

Mateo. Sorry, but I wasn't there two thousand years ago. Oh, you meant in the Bible, huh?

Jesus. Well, I was explaining it's in your soul. That's our connection with heaven.

Mateo. Cool. What if I lose the connection. Will I go "downstairs"?

Jesus. Don't worry. Just be nice and try to do the right thing. You'll make it.

Mateo. If I do, will I see you up there?

Jesus. Maybe, but I'm super busy. Don't worry, though. I have a group of coworkers who do what I do. There's a line in the Bible about that too.

Mateo. What about the soul living in the body thing?

Jesus. Yes, we are all souls living in a body. Usually, though, our personality gets in the way, and the soul doesn't come through much.

Mateo. Sounds kinda like me, dude.

Jesus. Now check out this part, Mateo. The whole gig is to get it together so that eventually—no rush—your personality becomes a perfect vehicle for your soul to express itself here on earth.

Mateo. This sounds kinda impossible, at least for me!

Jesus. That's why it takes so long. That's where the reincarnation piece comes into play.

Mateo. Okay, so I gotta ask you, if you don't mind: Are you, like, Hindu or something?

Jesus. Nope, not me. I'm about Truth. Religion is for people. Religion is a way to understand and practice spirituality. Some folks started a religion after I was around last time. That was helpful. There's stuff about living more than once in the Bible too.

Mateo. Really?

Jesus. Sure, dude. Sorry, I mean, Mateo. Check out where it says John the Baptist was once the prophet Elijah.

Mateo. Gotcha, but I'll have to order a Bible since I don't have a copy. You think Amazon has it?

Jesus. I have to go in a minute, so here it is in a nutshell: Do what you need to do to let your light shine. That light is the Universe within us. Always let your conscience be your guide. Do the right thing, because what goes around comes around. Be nice. Help others. Feel the love.

Mateo. I hear you, Jeez. Hey, sorry, now that we met, was it okay that I just used your nickname?

Jesus. Call me whatever you want, Mateo, and I'll plan to see you "upstairs." I'll leave you with this question to contemplate, Mateo. When you die and your whole life flashes before you, what will it take for you to be content?

Mateo. Ohhh. That will keep me up at night.

Jesus. I hope so.

Mateo. This was totally amazing, man! You gotta go, huh? You must have to work 24-7 at your job! I'm only doing forty hours a week. We could sure use more hard-working people like you, dude.

Jesus. They're coming. I don't work alone. Be ready. Adios, amigo.

Mateo. Adios, bro!

CHAPTER 14

Zune came over to see Neeya. When she asked him, he always offered useful ideas about what to do next or how to handle people. Most importantly, he was the main source of support for her, and she was profoundly grateful to him. With clear, sparkling blue eyes, wearing an untucked buttonless golden shirt and white cotton pants, he was a breath of fresh air for her. Being so handsome sure helped a lot too. Neeya had always tried to look nice for him but now was able to appreciate just being her casual self when he came over to visit—no need for makeup, jewelry, or colorful clothing. She wore loose-fitting turquoise-blue sweats today and was barefoot.

"Zune, I had no idea politics would become even more combative because of the Great Leaders thing. I see factions in Congress, and at state and local levels, where corrupt, unethical politicians are being heralded as saintlike people who are supposed to be the Great Leaders I talked about. What really disturbs me is the fanatical response to them. Now, there are a ton of these fake Great Leaders with people willing to follow them. It's so sad."

"Seems to me, Neeya, your message is not actually about the Leaders themselves. It's about their ideas, their energy, and how we really can change the world for the better. That's what galvanizes people. It stimulates us to see things in a new way, inspiring us to act accordingly. The Great Souls will not do the work; we will."

"That reminds me, Zune, of that cliché, 'Talk won't cook the rice.'"

"Yep," Zune replied with a grin. "It's our actions which count the most. Just keep on moving forward, getting the For the Common Good project going, and I'm sure you will be on the right track, Neeya."

"I can't see how I can ever repay you for all you have been doing, Zune," she said with soft, heartfelt earnestness.

"Just be yourself. Do what you know in your heart you can do. That will be my payback."

"I love you, Zune." He smiled his love back at her.

"Who sent you, Zune?" she asked again, truly meaning it, as if there was some greater plan he was serving.

"Maybe you did, Neeya." They laughed together during another of their wordless, heartfelt, yet platonic embraces.

Despite her growing focus on gathering coworkers for the project on the common good and relentless emails about the videomentary, Neeya still could not stay away from the news for very long. She remained determined not to let enthusiasm for the new project distract her but was successful only some of the time.

Neeya tuned into an all-news station on her TV. *It's more of the same, only worse each day. Gee, I hope it's not too late for some real leaders or for the common-good initiative to make a difference.*

It was hard for Neeya to believe the unemployment rate and inflation were both so incredibly high at the same time. Even if you had enough money, it was still hard to get a lot of what you wanted. Supply chain shortages and the loss of so many businesses which just couldn't keep up with all the challenges were all too prevalent. But what was really becoming the major issue was the social unrest. It was spilling over into the streets. Stores, and people, too, were getting robbed. It had become common to see angry protests in front of banks and government buildings.

Looting was becoming widespread. Many looters thought the injustices caused by inequity and a chronic inability to access resources justified taking what was not theirs. Even so, many of the stores being looted were owned by individuals, not big corporations. *I can understand looting a grocery store if you need food, have no money, and the food pantries are also empty, but stealing clothing, cell phones, microwave ovens, and even cars—that's way different!*

Even more troubling was the imminently catastrophic impact of the massive glacier shelf which had fallen into the ocean. The turbulence of the ocean and the damage to boats and harbors was bad enough itself. It was the vast waves of water—yes, the water seeking to submerge the earth's coastal areas—which was so hard to fathom. Waves of waves. Most people were not really able to see the danger coming or have any idea how to prepare themselves. Some cities were using adaptation, such as sandbags or building seawalls, to try and hold back what was coming. Island nations were especially vulnerable to overwhelming flooding and had less resources to cope. Neeya knew she was avoiding the magnitude of the danger heading toward us any day now, often feeling powerless about it.

Neeya turned off the TV, not allowing herself to check out the coverage on other stations, fearing more of the same distressing news. It was time to get ready and head out for another meeting with people who had the interest and skills to work with her on the For the Common Good project. She couldn't wait to get it beyond the realm of ideas and concepts into a practical reality.

Trying to shift into a positive mood, Neeya chose a slim, ankle-length dress with dark-blue and pink colors. She even rubbed some blush on her cheeks to help make herself feel a little rosy. Her straight brown hair was tied back in a loose ponytail. Sneakers were replaced by low black heels, nails painted purple. Neeya was highly motivated to run a productive business meeting with her new colleagues. She was glad Kim took the afternoon off to join her in this new effort.

Emerging from her apartment building, Neeya was relieved to see that protestors were no longer harassing her. She stopped at an electronics store to get a SIM card for her new cell phone. Neeya was greeted at the counter by a young Asian woman whose smile was a bright counterpoint to the despairing current events.

"Very good morning! How can I help you?"

"Hi. I need an international SIM card for my Samsung S31 phone," Neeya replied.

"Ha!" The woman's smile transformed into a derisive laugh. Neeya was taken aback.

"What do you mean 'ha'?" wondered Neeya aloud.

"Don't you know about the shortage of electronic parts?"

"I do, but how long a wait are we talking about?"

"Ha! How am I supposed to tell you if the manufacturers and distributors are not telling me? Maybe a few weeks, maybe a few months, maybe never. Ha!"

Neeya quietly stood still as the man in line behind her overheard the conversation and became agitated. He began yelling at the employee, blaming her for the shortages. The intensity of his anger made Neeya very uncomfortable. Realizing any kind of attempted intervention now was a no-win situation, she quickly headed for the door.

After such an unnerving experience at the electronics store, Neeya decided to take an extra-long route to her meeting. *I need to walk!* She headed toward the subway in order to avoid passing the area near Columbus Circle. It had become the site of daily protests, which were increasingly volatile. Right-wing extremists appeared there daily as their vehemence grew stronger. Far-left liberals and "peacemakers" were present to counter them. Law enforcement officers placed themselves in between the two groups, but fights broke out anyway, and people were injured. It often became virtually impossible for bystanders to determine what issues people were actually complaining about.

Each side had grown to distrust and despise the other side. Some "peacemakers" were themselves unable to remain peaceful, becoming just as indignant as the protestors. *It's worth it to go way out of my way just to avoid all this insane chaos!*

Neeya passed the subway entrance to the downtown tracks. The stairway was blocked by a barrier with yellow tape. The two police officers in front of the barricade were the targets of intense verbal abuse from people demanding the situation be fixed "immediately." It took Neeya just a moment to read the hastily posted sign, hear the angry voices, and pull out her cell phone. A foot of salty ocean water had entered the subway system, and most trains in the city had suddenly stopped running. The pumps belowground could not keep up with the inflow of ocean water. What got pumped out just came right back inside.

It was the realization that life as we knew it really was ending which stopped her in her tracks. There was crisis after crisis of such tremendous proportion that it was all now fusing into one profound crisis—a crisis of a world no longer able to function, no longer able to allow us to continue as we had been living. We were warned about these crises for decades, but few paid enough attention. Most of us assumed "they" would take care of it or simply avoided the issues altogether. Now, it was too late for avoidance. New ways of living have to be created today, and Neeya was determined to be a productive part of the effort.

Nero fiddled while Rome burned, but I gotta do something. Even if it's just a drop in the bucket, a million drops can fill an awfully big bucket. If those Great Leaders don't show up soon, we're done for. And what about the Prism? I'm waiting...!

Zune arrived at Neeya's apartment at 7:00 p.m.—exactly on time, as always. She wanted to tease him about an OCD-like tendency but appreciated the promptness and his way of being so smooth and present, always at the right place at the right time. She couldn't resist teasing him anyway.

"Gee, Zune, what happened to you? The 7:00 p.m. chime rang almost a minute ago."

"Oh, I guess you didn't realize Neeya. I haven't become perfect—yet," he chuckled. *Why am I thinking he* will *be perfect one day soon?*

Neeya told Zune about her meeting earlier today. She exuded excitement over a new group of coworkers coalescing around a vision of the common good. He was pleased to hear this. As the primary emotional source of support for Neeya and her endeavors, he nourished her in this special way of his.

They enjoyed a dinner of Thai, green curry chicken takeout plus two dishes Neeya cooked to go along with it. Zune especially liked the taste of a stir-fry with brussels sprouts and string beans she prepared using fresh ginger and garlic. Zune brought a bottle of chenin blanc wine, which went well with the meal. After this unique pairing of food, Greek halvah was a treat for dessert, providing their palates with a much-appreciated sweet finish to a savory meal.

After some light chitchat, Neeya noticed Zune had a faraway look in his eyes. His demeanor had changed too. He seemed serious.

"What's up, Zune?" she asked him very directly.

"It's that time, Neeya." She knew he wasn't talking about the 9:00 p.m. news.

"Go on, please." The tone of her voice revealed anxiousness arising within her.

Zune paused a moment. "The future is calling, and I must go."

"Go?" She knew it was bound to happen one day but didn't expect it right now.

"Yes, Neeya. To quote the great American poet Walt Whitman: 'Forever to know the universe itself as a road, as many roads, as roads for traveling souls, alive, forever forward. Strong and content, I travel the open road.' It's my Journey on the Infinite Highway of Life."

Hearing Zune deliver these lines in such a clear, strong, and earnest voice, Neeya knew it was hopeless to challenge him. Talking him out of leaving had zero chance of success. Her chin drooped downward, tears silently bathing her cheeks. She could not speak for a couple of minutes. Zune patiently joined her in the silence.

"I hear you, Zune, but please explain why you are leaving now when so much is happening and there is so much to do?"

"Neeya, my destiny always lies ahead. I do what I can when I pause along the way, as I have done here with you. Now, I must continue this Journey of mine. No map is needed along the Infinite Highway. The next stop is always the right one. I am able to sense when to get off the open road and give what help I can to the people in the situations I find. It's about being of service."

"But will you come back here, Zune?" she asked with a note of desperation.

"I am always going forward, Neeya," he answered softly, taking her hands.

Neeya drew in an easy, full breath, exhaling it in a slow, shuddering sigh. Her anxious sadness departed with the air, allowing her heart to be freed of sorrow, replenishing it with the joy of time spent with Zune. Their time together was her most special gift. As usual, his silent smile conveyed understanding.

They stood there face-to-face, his hands holding hers. *It will be so hard to go on without you, Zune.*

"Don't fret, Nee. There will be other sources of support." *Is he reading my mind again?*

"I am just starting the group work for the common good. There is so much to do."

"There sure is. I am sure you will do it, and much good will come of it."

"I hope so, but it's hard to imagine doing it without you, my Zune."

He took Neeya's arms, gently pulling her close, their faces only inches apart.

"You are never alone, Neeya. And hey, what about those Muses from your dreams? You told me they are real. Well, trust that, and be open to the inspiration."

She gazed into the depths of his eyes, sensing his soul as an endless, living well. *I can get lost there forever.* Zune inched forward, their foreheads gently uniting. Neeya felt his presence so deeply within her heart, a loving compassion blessing every cell in her being. *Oh my God, I know this vibe. It's the same energy as the Muses. He must be connected with them.*

"Great Leaders really are emerging. Thanks to you, Neeya, many millions now expect them. This will help humanity be receptive to their presence and their work. They will not announce themselves as leaders. They will simply and totally excel in their own fields of activity. They will inspire and lead. Humanity will do the work."

"I hope you're right, Zune" was Neeya's humble response. *May my dreams come true!* "But will people know that they really are... well, great?"

"Yes, they will. These Great Souls have the highest level of integrity and character. They have no wrong inclinations or bad habits. And it won't just be about them. They will support and work through individuals and groups who do good work, those who are seen as experts in their own fields."

"Can you say a little more about them, Zune?"

"These men and women who are the Great Ones will be examples of selfless service. They will encourage right attitudes toward material living."

"Zune, what about the one I call the Prism?"

"He is *the* Great One."

"Is he really coming too?"

"Yes. I refer to him as the Coming One." Neeya got the chills.

"Zune, please tell me." Neeya was almost pleading. "Will I see you again?"

"If we follow the impulses of our own souls, our paths will cross."

"How do I know which is the right path?"

"Trust yourself. Listen to your conscience and follow it as best you can. When you know in your heart what you must do, then do it no matter what. When obstacles arise or doubt and fear rear their ugly heads, do not be deterred. Strive onward. Trust your heart. Trust your Muse. Stay on your path of Truth."

Foreheads touching, hands intertwined, their souls blended, they stood silently in their hearts' embrace. Neeya would eventually come to realize they did stay connected.

I love you, Zune! She was too emotional to speak.

"I love you too, Neeya." Now she knew what kind of love he was talking about—not a romantic love. *How can my heart feel sad and be filled with so much love at the same time?* Neeya wondered.

Moments later, Zune resumed his Journey on the Infinite Highway of Life, his everlasting way.

CHAPTER 15

Whenever the day dawned to resume his Journey on the Infinite Highway of Life, Zune heard the same familiar phrase sounding in his mind: "Forever to know the universe itself as a road, as roads for traveling souls, alive, forever forward. Strong and content, I travel the open road."

As the open road irresistibly beckoned, Zune became inspired and compelled to continue his Journey. Successfully accomplished opportunities heralded a new phase soon to manifest. The underlying theme at each destination was served by effectively managing the plot unfolding there.

Zune often thought traveling the Infinite Highway was an interlude between detours, like Bleakville and New York. Sometimes it seemed the opposite, as if the detours were the interludes. Eventually he came to accept them both as aspects of the one Journey, and you can't have one without the other. Traveling the Infinite Highway, his soul was refreshed and deepened by experiences along the eternal Way. Zune had come to see "the universe itself as a road." He welcomed the Journey with every fiber of his being.

I will ride this road ever forward, trusting to take the right turnoff and make the most of it, no matter what may arise before me. I will stay connected with my Muse.

The Infinite Highway is a road so steep, travelling it requires the utmost of one's inner resources. The longer one traveled this path, the greater one's will, heart, and mind strengthened and expanded. The number of those long on this Journey were few. Fortunately, there were some who had advanced exceedingly far along this path. Perhaps it was a way to become a Great Soul.

Zune wondered who had traveled the Infinite Highway the longest. This person may have become what it takes to be the one Neeya calls the Prism.

As turnoffs on this road are very scarce, Zune learned to be patient and trust his intuition to recognize the one meant for him. It was late in the afternoon when he saw the sign - Transcendent Valley. For a moment it seemed a bit pretentious, yet he hoped the name was actually an auspicious one. *Either way, I am going there and will soon find out.*

Leaving the low, rolling, arid upland of the plains behind him, Zune's car gained altitude, entering green, wooded hills. It was late spring here and the fresh fragrance of leaves on trees caught his attention. The terrain slowly steepened. Vistas grew greater. Hills transformed into mountains, their granite, rocky peaks proudly beckoning above as he reached the tree line. At the highest elevations above him snow and ice covered the mountain tops. The turquoise hue of an icy outcrop revealed a glacier, silently living there since the last ice age, moving steadily along at its infinitely slow pace.

Reaching the pass on a shoulder of the highest peak, Zune pulled over to take in the scope of the magnificent panorama. Enough daylight remained to gift him a glimpse of the sun's vivid illumination enhancing the rich tints of earth and sky. Zune looked back, beyond from where he had come, gazing into the boundless distance of the past.

Zune turned around to face a future waiting below in a most beauteous verdant valley, rung by these majestic mountains. A turquoise river, born of melting snow and ice from above, wove its way along the valley floor, nurturing all life surrounding its path. Zune stood there for a long time, absorbing it all deeply. He felt the vibrant peace radiating from the valley, calling to his soul as if some kind of cosmic magnet. Zune was absolutely sure he had taken the right turnoff.

A few moments later, he was back in his car, gradually descending the winding road and entering the valley. Zune became infused with the joy of being in the right place at the right time. *I'm ready,* he avowed.

Almost halfway down into the valley, Zune stopped again, wanting one more grand view. Observing the valley floor in more detail, he was puzzled by its unusual orderliness. Zune noticed that the fields, meadows, and orchards had borders lacking the straight lines and perimeters commonly seen in places like England. This puzzled him until he realized the roads, gardens, and fields were all crafted to follow the natural contours of the land. He thought of it as the ultimate feng shui landscape. Even the buildings themselves were constructed so their contours meshed with the local topography. He admired the way this fluid symmetry simply felt so good to behold.

Zune observed the lack of a concentrated, dense downtown area. The small town spread out rather evenly along the bottom of the valley, with plenty of room between buildings, many of which were topped with a greenish substance he could not identify. Zune could not see any telephone poles, cell towers, or electric lines. In three places, he saw buildings organized in geometric patterns resembling a circular grid, expanding out from one larger central structure. Zune was most intrigued, realizing there was an integrated purpose here which he had yet to fully grasp.

Now, it was time to get back in his car to experience this special valley close up and meet its inhabitants. His reason for being there would soon present itself. *It always does when I travel the Infinite Highway of Life.*

Zune drove slowly, passing people clearly content, playing, strolling along, or working on their clean, colorful homes and properties. There were very few cars yet plenty of bikes moving along a parallel path as wide as the one for motorized vehicles.

Zune felt that old, familiar yearning for some lime seltzer and was on the lookout for a local source of his favorite thirst-quencher. Little did he know that another long-deferred, sublimated thirst would soon be sated too. Zune stopped in front of the Venerable Valley Deli, having been on the road for what felt like ages. Maybe it had been. Either way, it was so good to get out of his car. He looked forward to meeting new people. Zune never felt alone as he drove along by himself, but here in this special valley, he was again ready to be a part of something more.

Moments later, he saw her. Composed and alert, she stood there, a compelling figure, dressed in green shorts, a yellow T-shirt, and white sneakers, dark-blond hair flowing behind her. Naylu had just finished her daily five-mile morning run and was back in town behind the deli.

She delighted in the undulating flow of a stream offering her water clean and pure enough to drink. Dipping her cup, she imbibed gratefully.

A natural-born leader with a wonderful blend of strength and compassion, her spirit enthused and uplifted those in her presence. Her words of guidance were considered wise and practical. Naylu was humble and real—no bloated ego here. She was full of useful ideas, easily striking a chord of agreement with her neighbors. When she facilitated a meeting of community members, a vote was rarely needed due to her skill in coalescing group thought and reaching consensus. Naylu had an innate ability to show up at the right place at the right time—just like Zune.

Refreshed, Naylu stood still upon the grassy bank, at peace and so alive. Aware of a pleasant stirring within, she let herself quietly experience this new, enchanting vibe for a moment. Its unique quality felt somehow familiar. Naylu sensed its source. Turning around, she saw him standing nearby, gazing out across the valley at the mountains beyond. Intuitively, without an iota of questioning or hesitancy, Naylu began moving toward him. Zune turned to face her as she approached, instantly aware the future had become the present.

"Hi there," said Naylu, though her presence had already greeted him. Zune immediately cherished her smile, so bright and lovely.

"And hi to you," he was able to say after a moment. "I've been on the road a very long time. It feels like ages since I've spoken to anyone. This is a great way to start."

"Then welcome to our special valley."

"Gazing down from the mountain pass, I could tell this truly is a special valley. There is something extraordinary here."

"There sure is. So what brings you here?"

"That's to be determined." Zune briefly told her about his Journey on the Infinite Highway and the inner, intuitive impulse to take the turnoff which led him there.

"I knew someone was coming," she replied gently, averting her eyes for just a moment.

"I wish I could say I knew someone was waiting."

They held eye contact silently and then exchanged names. Naylu and Zune extended their hands in greeting exactly at the same time. Pressing their palms together, it was as if they were downloading an amorphous montage of each other's soul. There was no need to ask the typical questions about the who, what, and where of their lives. These were moot points in the richness of this moment.

Naylu nodded toward the stream and began to walk in its direction. Zune joined her before she completed her first step. They meandered along a path softened by pine needles, warmed by the sun. Their auras blended easily. Several minutes passed before they spoke again. Zune did so first.

"It is so impressive the way houses are built with the contours of the land. Each house is different, but the shapes and colors, as well as the landscaping, make them all fit together so well—not like the rigidly structured sameness of a typical suburban town, with all predetermined straight lines. It feels so light and easy here."

"That is true," Naylu agreed. "Some people refer to it as good geomancy. And we don't use synthetic material like treated wood, aluminum siding, or unhealthy paint. Houses are oriented to get as much direct sun exposure as possible. This helps warm them, and with lots of windows, there is plenty of light inside. Buildings are situated so that rain and melting snow are harvested in large barrels. We use it for our gardens. The rest flows downhill into the river."

"I've never seen so many nut trees before. Hickory, pecan, hazelnut, walnut…wow," Zune replied with surprise. "They all look healthy, well pruned, and so productive!"

"I'm impressed that you can recognize them. Why import nuts from foreign countries at high prices when we can grow them here for free? Between the mountain snowmelt feeding our river, enough rain, and a deep well for each home, we do just fine. Fertilizer is made of natural byproducts from other things we grow or use, but it's also free, and we avoid toxic chemicals," Naylu explained.

Zune looked around and saw the homes were surrounded by berry bushes and flowers, all looking flush and ripe. Naylu answered his question before he asked it.

"By matching our landscaping with the flora and soil, a prosperous companionship has developed. The bees, birds, and bugs pollinate and disperse seeds. They have plenty of food of their own without eating what we are growing and no reason to bite or sting us. Crop rotation and companion planting help maintain healthy soil. We are stewards of Gaia."

"Looks and sounds great."

"Sure is. We can't control nature, but we have learned to live in harmony with it. That took a long time, but now, we are mostly in balance with nature, and this works just fine for all of us."

"Please tell me about the gardens, Naylu. Seems like every house has one."

"We mostly eat only what we grow or raise ourselves. For some of the larger crops, like wheat, corn, and oats, we have fields and community gardens with large plots, which many of us tend together. Everyone's basic need for food is met. Folks can grow whatever else they may want on their own. We do bring in things like salt and other seasonings, as well as some oils. There is usually no cost for this. We trade with items we produce, which other communities may not have."

"Are you folks vegetarian?"

"Many of us are. Some folks eat fish or poultry. We make our own cheese with milk from our cows or goats. We catch fish from local streams and rivers or Diamond Lake a few miles away. I don't think anyone hunts anymore, but they can if they want."

"What about clothing?"

"We make a lot of it ourselves, especially using wool from sheep and llamas we raise."

"This is all very impressive," Zune acknowledged.

"We also trade services within our community and with some other nearby towns. A really efficient system of bartering has developed. We use bartering for so many of our goods and services, there is a limited need for the use of money."

"That's cool, Naylu. The need for money has governed the lives of millions for so many centuries. It tends to be a tool of selfishness and greed. Using money produces so much inequity. There are better ways to manage the exchange of goods and services."

"Those days of craving more and more material things or money are mostly gone here in this valley, thank goodness. But please understand, we are not ascetics."

"So are you folks producing more than you use here?" Zune inquired.

"Yes, especially with food. After we have traded and bartered for what we need, we share the excess with food pantries in a larger nearby town. We do bring in some revenue from the sale of other things, like the extra furniture we craft, and we donate that money to a few small medical clinics in the region. Then people with no health insurance or little money can get medical care for free."

"That's wonderful, Naylu."

"Thanks, Zune. We do hope that we are creating a community able to serve as a model for other towns."

Naylu and Zune spent the early twilight getting to know each other over sandwiches from the Venerable Valley Deli and a walk along a countryside road.

"How long will you be staying here, Zune?"

"I rarely have an agenda or a timeline for when I arrive at a destination. Situations just seem to develop, and I try to be useful. But hey, I have absolutely no inclination to leave here and move on anytime soon."

"Do you have a place to stay?"

"Besides setting up a tent next to my car and camping out?" Zune half-jokingly answered.

"We have a few small guest cottages. I know of one very close by which is available."

"I'd be crazy to decline that offer. Thanks so much, Naylu."

"It is truly my pleasure, Zune." Her voice was direct, soft, and warm. They both sensed the inevitable, unsure how or when it might manifest.

Zune was intrigued by how Naylu could be such a gentle soul yet have such apparent inner strength and poise. She exuded a very strong feminine force. Unthreatened, Zune welcomed it. *What a woman! Maybe she was a warrior goddess in another life.*

The cabin was cozy, warm, and immaculately clean, with just enough furnishings to make it comfortable. Zune sat back on the easy rocking chair, eyes resting upon the fully leaved, lofty, rugged ash trees standing tall before him. He took a quick moment to remember his last stop in that big city—a chaotic realm reverberating with numerous crises and tensions. Here in this special valley, it felt so harmonious, yet he was sure there was more to the story. Zune relinquished thoughts of the past as well as those of tomorrow, letting his mind clear.

I need to get this right. The future will present itself tomorrow. I could easily stay here for a long time. He still sensed Naylu's presence within him. *I wonder what the universe has in store.*

At first glance, all seemed especially well here, although he had barely scratched the surface. Zune had been traveling the Infinite Highway for so long, he was in no rush to find out. Stillness was the theme right now, and he sank deeply into it.

Neeya and her visions of the Muses and the Prism appeared to Zune's inner eye as his consciousness drifted off into abstract realms. Becoming swathed in sleep, there was no time to consider why Naylu's presence may have evoked a vision of the Prism.

Zune awoke at dawn after a long, peaceful rest, feeling refreshed and clear. Naylu had left exceptionally tasty corn muffins with homemade butter and freshly roasted coffee, making for a most satisfying breakfast. Zune looked forward to meeting with Naylu again in the afternoon for a walk in this unique community.

On this sunny, warm morning with its choir of birdsong and a bubbling stream, there was no way Zune was going to remain inside. He ate his breakfast outside, sitting in a hand-carved cedar rocking chair, absorbing the peacefulness permeating the valley. He was surprised to see rabbits, turkey, and deer meandering so close to him with their welcoming glint, as if to say, "Good morning, new person."

Soon, a woman approached, walking slowly, looking directly at him, her gaze never wavering. Zune was comfortably receptive to this unexpected arrival, wondering what was about to unfold.

Tall, slender, and light-brown-skinned, her black braids tied with deep-purple ribbons cascaded down beyond the length of her back. She reminded him of a Native American princess or medicine woman, given her rather noble demeanor. He felt no need to inquire. Her presence was revealing the answer.

"Greetings, Zune. I am Aiyana. Naylu told me about you and encouraged me to visit."

"So nice to meet you, Aiyana. My first visitor!"

"I heard you were very impressed with our lovely valley. Would you like to stroll around and learn some more about it?"

"Sure, Aiyana. That sounds wonderful. Thanks so much."

"Good. We can walk as soon as you are ready."

"Let's go, please. How nice it is to experience the proximity and friendliness of the animals here."

"Ah, yes, I do like to think of them as our friends."

Aiyana went on to explain, "We live in a cooperative existence with the mineral, vegetable, and animal kingdoms. It's the only way to go if you want nature to work with you. We now have cleaner rivers, our microclimate is changing for the better, and there is little to no pollution. A lush, orderly abundance of healthy life exists here. We are one with nature and all life. We keep it simple and have found ways to make use of the earth's resources without depleting them."

"That sounds just right, Aiyana. Humanity has mostly forgotten it is part of nature, not separate from it."

"True. And we strive to be consciously aware of experiencing it, always."

From a well deep in the repository of long-forgotten memories, Zune recalled a line from a Native American song and recited it aloud: "The earth is our mother; we must take care of her."

"You've got it," replied Aiyana, pleasantly surprised.

"Please go on," Zune requested.

"We have a deep reverence of the feminine principle so much at the heart of what nature is all about. This awareness has been all but lost in recent centuries due to the usurping of the planet's resources for selfish use. We are so much more in touch with the physical world here, and it responds really well to our stewardship.

"Humanity has long been pretty much out of balance with the natural world. We have had mostly patriarchal, male-governed societies, and one can make the argument that they are often unsuccessful, at least in the long run. There are several reasons for this. One is an insufficient openness of heart, as the focus is usually overly cerebral and self-centered. Another is a lack of reverence for the earth and for women."

"I sure have seen plenty of those almost everywhere, and material and territorial greed are other factors," Zune replied.

"Well, Zune, here, the pendulum is swinging into balance. Men as well as women participate in our seasonal and other rituals honoring the feminine principle. Men do not feel threatened by the new balance of male and female energies. Women are more able to be fully open in their relations with men, due to a much higher level of respect which men now have for women. Women here are often found in leadership positions."

"Ah. Makes sense to me. Reminds me of how it was in some of the Native American cultures before Europeans came to this continent."

"That's right, Zune. Some tribes had women in the dominant roles.

"Most of us here are in good moods nearly all the time. It's not just that our way of life is so much less stressful. We have a more insightful understanding of what mental health is, and we are able to recognize emotional issues and deal with them proactively. Psychiatric medications are rarely used. For schizophrenia or severe bipolar disorder, which are actually medical illnesses of the brain, we often do use medication. We are supportive of each other, and you don't see much denial or avoidance here.

"We spend a lot of time outside in the sun, breathing fresh, vitalizing, clean air. We encourage adjustments in diet, improvement in physical health, and early attention to medical needs. We also try to determine the cause of illnesses rather than treating only symptoms. As you can see, we are focused on prevention."

Aiyana continued her tour, stopping before a large patch of blueberries and raspberries adjacent to a small grove of peach trees. She plucked a peach, cutting it in half with a small ceramic pocketknife. Zune picked some berries. He was caught off guard by how quickly Aiyana reached out to gently touch the back of his hand just before the berries entered his mouth.

"We always take a moment before we eat."

"Oh, yes, Aiyana," he said humbly.

"We have deep gratitude and respect for Mother Earth and the gifts she produces. Everything that lives is holy, so we live accordingly." Zune repeated her words, and Aiyana was pleased to see he meant it. Zune was delighted to experience such totally ripe, large, flavorful berries. After a while, they were back at his cottage.

"Aiyana, please accept my deep gratitude for showing me around this paradise. What a wonderful place is this valley." She chuckled at his earnest expression.

"Well, Zune, it's not a paradise yet, but maybe we can get there one day. It is precious here, but we are far from perfect. And the world around us is so imperfect. If you stay for a while, there's a lot more to learn."

"I'm sure I won't be leaving anytime soon." That comment of his brought Naylu strongly to mind.

"Then I'm sure I'll see you again, Zune."

"I hope so, and thanks so much again for coming to visit, Aiyana."

She departed, her gait strong and slow. Zune settled back down in the cedar rocker, spending the next hour digesting the experience of his time with Aiyana and the gifts of this valley.

CHAPTER 16

Zune walked along the road, humming an old Irish folk tune. People he passed along the way made and held eye contact, offering pleasant greetings. *It's so easy to like it here and feel at home.*

Zune realized that other than one pickup truck and a car, he had not seen any other large vehicles on the road today. There were several people driving what looked like EV golf carts, which made minimal noise. *Maybe that's one reason why it's so quiet around here.*

Zune stopped to admire the shape of a large white building, gently gleaming in the sunlight. Its roof and sides were a continuous curved arc from its apex to the ground. He noticed a band of light-gray panels around its circumference and stood there wondering what they were.

Just then, a man emerged from the building, noticing Zune's inquisitive gaze.

"Hi there; I couldn't help but notice your curiosity about this building. I can tell you were wondering about its construction. Would you like me to shed some light on it?"

"Sure."

The man was pleasant and articulate, giving the impression of having much knowledge on the subject. He was of Asian descent with closely cropped black hair, black eyes, and a short, sturdy build.

"This is our central community building. The walls are made of natural thermochromic materials which can adjust their color in relation to light and temperature. In hotter weather, the hue is white, reflecting the heat to stay cool. During colder days, the hue becomes darker, almost black, retaining the sun's heat really well."

"That's so innovative. What are the panels across its midsection and roof?"

"They are photovoltaic solar panels, and since their batteries have exceptional storage capacity, the system can fully power our building year-round." His smile was not one of pride, but rather one of joy in the efficiency of their advanced technology.

"We are very grateful to essentially be off the grid. In fact, we produce more than we use. The surplus of electricity we generate then gets fed into the grid, and we get credits for it. The credits are given to folks in neighboring towns who can't afford to pay all of their electric bills."

"That's a very practical example of energy efficiency," said Zune.

"So, sir, I assume you are Zune, the man Naylu told me about this morning."

"Yes, I am. How can you tell?"

"Well, I haven't seen you around here before, plus, your attire is what some might call a bit outmoded, friend," he replied, smiling broadly.

"Gee, I never thought of myself that way, but I guess it's true now," laughed Zune. This made him wonder again just how long his last ride on the Infinite Highway really had been.

"My name is Tashi. So glad we had a chance to meet."

"Me too, Tashi." Zune liked him a lot right away, especially his sincere friendliness. "I once knew a man by the same name, Tashi. He was from eastern Nepal."

"My lineage is from Tibet. My ancestors left Tibet with the Dalai Lama when he escaped to India after the Chinese invaded in 1959. I was born in the US, but I feel Tibet and the Himalayas in my soul. It infuses my sense of who I am. Hopefully, Tibet will be independent and free again one day."

"I hope so too, Tashi. Can you please tell me some more about the technical aspects of the infrastructure in this community?"

Tashi went on to describe how energy needs were resourced from solar panels, several wind turbines, and a small hydroelectric plant just below the falls of the river downstream from town. "A few of us have woodstoves. I love a wood fire, but the smoke impacts the quality of the air here. Most of us have high-efficiency heat pumps or use geo-thermal sources. No fossil fuels needed here."

Tashi explained, "Almost all clothing and furniture is made locally, as well as many of our tools and furnishings. Most of us learn some kind of craft or other skill we can use to contribute to the life of the community. We strive to be sure that all of us have our basic needs met. Beyond that, people can be creative in whatever way they choose. There is quite a bit of trade with other communities for items and materials that are not available to us locally."

Zune was impressed, complimenting Tashi on the community being a great example of living sustainably. "It took us a few generations, Zune. People here are pleased with their lives. That's what really counts!"

"What a place, Tashi. I admire how you folks are succeeding in manifesting your intentions."

"Yes. We have sports here, too, and while there certainly is some competition, it is in a friendly way. People can handle not winning. We just want to have fun, play hard, and get some good exercise."

"Way to go."

"Thanks. Excuse me, but it's time to go see my little granddaughter Kelsing. How about joining Naylu and I tomorrow so we can connect some more?"

Zune saw into the depths of Tashi's eyes, intuitively sensing an intention to discuss matters deeper than solar power or handmade clothing. Zune gladly accepted the invitation. They went their ways, each feeling like they had just begun a special friendship.

As Zune was drifting off to sleep later in his cozy guest cottage, a glimpse of Neeya's dreams appeared to his inner eye. In a round room bathed in a soft blue glow, the seven Muses sat. They were receiving an intense, enriching radiance emanating from the Prism and then transmitting it out into the world. Zune's spirit was greatly infused as he transitioned into sleep before he had time to think about the experience. When he awoke in the morning, the feeling was still with him. Zune wondered again why it had happened now as he imagined encountering one of the Great Leaders here in Transcendent Valley.

Naylu and Tashi stood outside the central community building on the morning of another exquisitely sunny day. Approaching them, Zune wondered, *Is it ever cloudy here?*

"We just love these sunny mornings," Tashi exclaimed. "We like the occasional cloudy, rainy days, too, as they provide water the earth needs." Zune wondered if Tashi had picked up on what he was thinking. Didn't really matter—he had nothing to hide these days.

They sat in an alcove near the central area, sipping coffee and tea at a low table crafted of cherry-tree wood and embedded with intricately carved gold and green polished stones. Zune asked to hear more about the community, especially how people got along with each other.

Naylu explained how the theme of the common good was a core value guiding life in the community. "Goodwill infuses our interactions with each other. It is heartfelt and real. This enables us to cooperate with each other and really get things done. Embracing the common good includes supporting and fostering the lives of the individuals who comprise the community. Our individuality is maximized as each of us becomes a living cell in the body of the community."

Zune asked, "Do you have some form of governance here?"

"Yes," said Tashi. "We call it our Community Council. Each neighborhood selects a representative. There are fifteen of these. Three are the Council Focalizers."

"Who are they?"

Tashi smiled, saying, "You're looking at two of us, Zune. You already met the third Focalizer, Aiyana, though Naylu is our true leader here, even if she is too humble to acknowledge it." Tashi grinned, winking at Naylu.

"Oh. Well, given what I can see about you folks, I am not surprised!"

Zune and Naylu continued to share eye contact.

"What happens when there are disagreements?"

Tashi admitted, "This is no utopian paradise, Zune. We certainly do have disagreements on various issues. We address them rather than avoid them. We don't make power plays to get our own agendas through."

"So how does that actually work, Naylu?" Zune asked.

"It starts with open discussion. People are tolerant enough to let others express their opinions. We make a sincere effort to listen to each other. There is a lot of back and forth. Sometimes, when the conversation gets too polarized, a neutral person is asked to participate. This additional balancing force can usually mediate the conversation and help them reach an understanding—or at least an acceptance—of the other's point of view. Then an agreement can be developed more easily."

"Do you folks ever agree to disagree?"

"Sure. We just don't get angry about differences. This does wonders for community life," Tashi responded. "We make almost all our decisions by consensus. Everyone gets a chance to speak their mind as we think together toward a decision eventually acceptable to all. This can take a while occasionally, but the system is working extremely well. Compromise and cooperation are recognized necessities."

"What about the importance of each individual, if the main focus is on the community as a whole?"

Naylu answered, saying, "Our individuality is sacred. So is the life of the community, of which we are all a part. We are not perfect. This is a work in progress. One especially important factor is that we are incredibly supportive of each other. We are living the axiom that says 'It takes a village.'"

"Seems like it's working really well," commented Zune. Tashi and Naylu affirmed this with big, warm smiles, which Zune returned.

"It all sounds great, but aren't there people who don't want to participate in your community life?"

"Yes, there are," Naylu answered. "Not just here, but all over this region and beyond, there are still many who have not let go of the old ways of greed and materiality. Locally, most of them live beyond the valley or up in the mountains. They are pretty self-sufficient but lack many of the goods and amenities we have here. We do some trading with them but don't interact much otherwise."

"As you most likely know, Zune, much of the world is still in the throes of conflict and chaos. We have basically succeeded in finding a way to live meaningfully and creatively without having to participate much in so-called mainstream life," said Tashi.

"What about crime?"

"It is minimal, since we all have most of what we want. Sharing is a fundamental theme here, which we fully embrace. It makes an incredible difference," answered Naylu.

Tashi then told Zune about ones they call the Outliers. "They are people living nearby who are not part of our community. Sometimes they raid our crops or steal machinery and tools from us. We warn them the first time and offer ways to collaborate, but they usually decline. These folks tend to be selfish, mistrusting, and easily angered. They resent what they think is the power of the community."

"What happens if it gets serious or violent?"

"It is rare but does happen. Some have gotten violent. For those, we have had to hold them for a day or so until they are calm enough and willing to leave peacefully. If they are armed and violent, we almost always are able to disarm them. We do keep a minimal amount of firearms on hand for emergencies beyond our control."

"No jails or prisons?"

"Not here, but once every year or so, we have had to relocate a violent Outlier to a more highly structured town not too far from here. There, they are encouraged to learn ways to coexist with neighbors they detest—that's us—without resorting to theft or violence. It usually works, but not always. The large regional city a day's drive from here has jails for the most dangerous. Like you heard a few minutes ago, this is not a utopian paradise. Much of the world is still writhing in turmoil, yet we are able to avoid most of that here."

The three new friends then decided to take a short break, resulting in a silent stroll outside. Zune marveled at the vast array of blooming, sweet-smelling flowers along the path he strolled. His mind offered memories of life in the big city with Neeya and the political, economic, social, and climate crises. He wondered how much of all the strife continued, admiring how this community was able to flourish in such a troubled world.

Zune pondered on what Neeya may have been doing lately. Having resumed his Journey on the Infinite Highway of Life, he was uncertain exactly how long ago it was he had left Neeya to continue the Journey. In a strange way he could not explain, Naylu seemed to embody something of Neeya's essence.

When they arrived back at the central building, Naylu and Zune continued walking together. Their connection was growing stronger by the minute. Being in her presence was wonderful. She felt exceedingly simpatico with him. His heart came alive when he was with her, resting in its natural state: love. Zune tried at first to think of it as spiritually based love like with Neeya, yet he was unable to rationalize away his persistent romantic feelings. The two were not really incompatible, even though spiritually based love did not have to become romantic or sensual. Zune wondered in his mind if it was mutual, though he knew in his heart it was. After all, how else could he know this? The heart is where Naylu and Zune truly met.

Simultaneously, they both paused, turning to face each other. The amorous sentiments yearned to manifest physically at this point.

"Now?" asked Zune softly. "Yes," whispered Naylu. They embraced— on every level.

There was no need to talk about how to meld into this new relationship. They merely reveled in this precious moment. Letting nature take its course had worked out just right.

Upon returning to the central building later, Tashi and Aiyana were not surprised to see Zune and Naylu holding hands, talking, laughing, and kissing. It seemed like a perfect match—a love divine.

17 CHAPTER

A iyana joined them at the aromatic cherry-wood picnic table. The four friends found themselves sitting together again in deep conversation, feeling like kindred souls and coworkers. Aiyana had prepared iced tea infused with fireweed honey made by community beekeepers. They sipped it slowly, savoring its richness.

Zune remained curious about how this community fit in with the rest of the world. "I've been away, on the road, for what feels like a long, long time. Clearly, some major changes are occurring. From what I can gather, despite significant global issues remaining on many fronts, like climate catastrophes, food insecurity, and political divisiveness, more people are working together to decrease the intensity of the key crises. This is great. What I have yet to grasp is, How did this happen? What is allowing the easing of the distrust and negativity and motivating people to work together?"

"You did miss some major developments, Zune," Naylu told him with a grin. "And it is still so very far from being a perfect world. Here in this valley, we are at the cutting edge of civilization's transformation, but there is still plenty of misery and negativity in so much of the world. We feel it, painfully."

"So, what did I miss, folks?"

"It was the emergence of a handful of exceptionally remarkable people. These most special human beings are providing ideas and guidance which are incredibly insightful and useful in managing our multiple crises. They offer productive solutions. They encourage people to come together in the realization that we either try implementing new strategies or civilization as we know it will soon stop functioning. It is guidance, optional and consensual, not coercion of any sort. That's why they are called *Great Leaders*."

Zune got the chills when he heard those words again. "Great Leaders!" he earnestly repeated aloud. It almost sounded like a question too.

"Yes, exactly," replied Naylu. Tashi took it from there.

"There was a videomentary made a while back called *Great Leaders*. It predicted these uniquely exceptional folks will turn up to help out with the world's biggest problems. I guess it was prophetic, because it started happening a few years ago."

"Neeya!" exclaimed Zune, rising up half out of his seat.

"Yes," said Tashi with surprise. "That is the name of the woman who made that videomentary. You knew this somehow?" It was a question, but the answer was obvious.

Zune's attention turned toward Naylu as he told them he knew Neeya and had assisted her with the *Great Leaders* videomentary.

Now it was Naylu's turn to get the chills as she murmured, "Oh." She was locked in eye contact with Zune, a gentle ripple of awe coursing through them both. It was like a déjà vu experience where they couldn't tell the past from the future.

"Tell me more," Zune prodded. "Please explain how the Great Leaders have been able to actually make a difference."

Tashi continued while Naylu kept staring at Zune. He felt her without looking. It was a penetrating gaze, yet not uncomfortable at all.

"These Great Souls have not suddenly appeared out of nowhere. Over many years, each rose to the highest prominence in their own fields. Attention was drawn to them by the astonishing and effective quality of their work. Over time, they became widely known for their unique stature. They each have an exquisitely profound presence. In the last few years, they have been openly affirming the coordination of their work together. This was a lot for many people to digest, especially at first.

"There are seven of these so-called Leaders, but don't get me wrong— they were not elected. They have no authority. It is their genius insight and ability to offer practical suggestions which allow them to rise into leadership positions. Something so dramatically dynamic and heartfelt about them inspires and galvanizes people to be receptive to what they have to say and then to take action. That's why some say a Great Leader can also be called a Muse.

"These Great Souls radiate deep concern and compassion for others. They are examples of people who have no wrong inclinations and no bad habits. They are guided by entirely ethical motives and selfless service.

"Their input has become highly regarded by governmental, economic, and social organizations. Most people are willing to try their ideas, and it sure pays off. They are people actively working to bring order out of chaos. We were on the verge of a possible worldwide nuclear Armageddon, given that North Korea, Iran, and several terrorist groups got so close to actually using nuclear weapons. This would have forced the US, Israel, or NATO to respond accordingly. It could have been the end of all of us."

"Wow. So you said there were seven of them. Can you please tell me in what areas they are working now?"

"Okay, here you go," responded Tashi. "Politics, education, economics, the arts, science and technology, religion, plus the seventh one—creating new templates for organizations and the social order reflecting our higher qualities."

Zune paused to take it all in. "Makes sense. I guess this covers most areas. That's what Neeya foresaw. I was expecting it would happen but couldn't be totally sure when." He continued to feel Naylu's gaze with its exceptionally lovely vibe. Naylu realized that even though Zune needed an update, he was somehow a part of all that was transpiring.

Naylu further explained, "It's not just about the Great Leaders. It's all the work, in every field, which so many people are engaged in because of them. It's about people, communities, and organizations working together to implement their ideas. That's what is making the difference, even within the UN."

Zune closed his eyes, pausing for a moment. Images of war, pandemics, suffering, hunger, floods, and wildfires surfaced. It was exceedingly unpleasant, but he immediately let them go, avoiding any painful emotions connected with them. This was a heathy detachment.

Zune became even more curious about the Great Leaders, so he inquired further. "What are these Great Souls up to now?"

It was Aiyana's turn to respond. "We know they are part of an inner network now externalizing, a group existing since time immemorial. This might include people like Leonardo da Vinci, Pythagoras, Confucius, Mozart, Sojourner Truth, Franklin Roosevelt, Mother Teresa, Martin Luther King Jr., and the founders of religions. They are all part of the network, even if they were not consciously aware of it in that lifetime. Each of them showed up on the world scene to provide a certain impulse or creative genius to help humanity move forward in our knowledge and development.

"Until recently, they had no need to talk about their true stature or being part of a group—or inner network, if you want to call it that. They each just did their own thing in the world, providing extraordinarily helpful ideas and energy. The work of many thousands in various fields has been greatly enhanced by their contributions. These Great Souls are seen to be functioning on a higher level which others simply have not reached yet.

"Most people implement their ideas simply because they work out so successfully and are spot on at such a difficult time. Others distrust them, feeling they may have too much influence. These Great Souls now present in the world are speaking openly about aspects of their true nature, their connection with each other, and the inner network. Of course, many who hear this think it is a bunch of blasphemy."

"What about right now? What is next?" Zune asked her. It grew potently quiet before Aiyana answered.

"In the videomentary you helped with, there was a prophecy based on Neeya's dreams, about the one she called the Prism, the Muse of all the Muses, the Greatest Soul of All."

"Right. I definitely remember and have my own expectation about it."

Aiyana continued. "Well, after Neeya's videomentary went viral, there was a speech given at the UN in which a diplomat made a prediction that—"

"Theo!" interjected Zune.

"Yes," said Aiyana. "He forecast the imminent arrival of the so-called Coming One in his famously provocative UN speech." Zune humbly told them he was there and heard it in person. No need to tell them about the man with a knife.

It grew quiet again for a few minutes. Naylu spoke this time. "Zune, the three of us understand that the emergence of—well, let's use Neeya's term—the Prism, is about to happen."

Tashi explained to Zune, "A very close childhood friend, now in Karachi, Pakistan, has long been involved with large-scale international hunger and starvation relief. He works closely with Lakshmi Kerala. Lakshmi is said to be one of those seven who many call Great Leaders. People are amazed at his ability to galvanize what it takes to bring together massive amounts of resources in no time at all. What he is able to accomplish is virtually miraculous. He does not do this by himself. He works through groups which collaborate with other groups.

"Lakshmi has let my friend and his colleagues know that each of the seven Great Leaders is now telling people that the one you call the Prism will soon emerge into public view. He is already becoming known, though not necessarily as the Coming One yet. Soon, he will be given an opportunity to address the world, probably from the UN, even as early as next week."

Aiyana added, "My brother is a professor at the London School of Economics. He has the privilege of assisting Richard Emerson, a genius said to be one of the group of Great Leaders. In the last couple of years, Mr. Emerson also has been acknowledging the existence of these Great Souls and the networks which developed to support their work. Recently he stuck his neck out and encouraged us to be aware there is a profoundly special one coming and to expect the public emergence of the Prism really soon."

Naylu reminded them of the "rapidly growing level of expectancy around the world that such a being as the Prism will appear on the scene.

"It's not just coming from religious circles either. So many of the most respected people, from all walks of life, have been brave enough to share their expectations. True wisdom in leadership has been sorely lacking. Given the increasing acceptance of the existence of Great Souls, many are now willing to consider what the so-called Prism might have to say. And this makes it easier for the masses to be receptive and hopeful."

In a soft, earnest tone Aiyana said, "Zune, we are hearing that given the ultra-high level of respect for the seven Great Souls and the professional stature and effectiveness of those working with them, many media outlets will cover the event, if it actually does happen. It will be streamed widely and available on cable, broadcast TV, and the radio," said Naylu. "Many millions around the globe are really psyched at the possibility of seeing the Prism. These seven, well, Muses are now publicly referring to him as their Muse. Who knows? If he really does show up and lives up to our expectations, we can figure out what to call him then."

"Maybe we'll have to figure out what to call *her* then," offered Naylu with a wide grin. The others smiled, easily assuming it was in the realm of possibility it could be a woman.

Zune was clearly enthusiastic about the opportunity of seeing such a Great Soul speak. "I have often imagined the incredible impact of such an event," he fervently expressed. "It will be exceptionally galvanizing."

It grew quiet again as the friends reflected on what such a global event would look like. Though not shared aloud, they each envisioned a stupendous moment, a powerful spiritual impulse infusing humanity with a most special vibe. Zune envisioned a kind of planetary epiphany.

Naylu told him, "The three of us spoke shortly after you showed up here, and we concluded that your arrival at this time is no coincidence. Lo and behold, you have a direct connection to the event we expect is about to happen—a worldwide event of profound proportions."

"I sensed it too," Zune told them. Trusting their sincerity and integrity, Zune shared that during his drive on the Infinite Highway, he also dreamed of a global occurrence involving the Prism. The others nodded in understanding. Zune sensed they knew more than they let on, yet so did he. *Not everything has to be said aloud.*

The four friends began to plan how the community could prepare for the possible public appearance of a Coming One. They were realistic enough to know that should it actually happen, it wouldn't be all love and roses around the planet. Many would likely think the speaker was a fake, the Antichrist, or who knows what. That could produce its own problems. The friends agreed such an event would just be the beginning of a new and better time, not the end of the world or the Rapture, as many thought. For now, they decided to assume the best, maintaining a focus on the positive impact it could have for humanity.

Tashi said, "Life will still go on. Things are just going to start to get better as enough people from all walks of life spread goodwill and work together to make it happen."

"True, Tashi," replied Zune. "Goodwill can be vitalized and empowered to become a powerful force for good. We all can take responsibility, in some small way, for at least kindling the flames of goodwill."

CHAPTER 18

The word soon quickly spread worldwide. Sunday will be the day awaited in heightened anticipation by multitudes. Tashi and Naylu worked with community members to prepare for the event. A massive, ultra-high-def screen was set up in the main community center. Some people decided to tune in from their homes. Everyone was free to do whatever they wanted. Only three community members were too dubious to watch. No one challenged their decision. Free will is embraced here.

Around the planet, people planned to gather with family and friends in houses of worship or various locales where they could watch together. At the same time, there were demonstrations alleging the coming event was something dark or false, encouraging people not to watch, in stark contrast to those with hopes of something wonderful.

A billion or so people were off the grid with no idea this event was happening. Many others were disinterested or wary and would not watch. The four friends expected most of the billions who do tune in will find the experience to be far more than expected. A great wave of hope and expectancy surged around the galvanized globe.

In a small stone house in a village near Bodo on the coast of Norway, several families closely huddled around a TV.

At an intricately tiled mosque in Luxor, Egypt, hundreds of Muslims gathered to await the event, though some of them doubted the expected Imam Mahdi would appear any place other than Mecca.

In northern India, not far from the holy mountain Nanda Devi in the Himalayas, Hindus and Buddhists met together in a pine grove between their temples, forgoing decades of mutual antagonism, wondering if they would see their Expected One today.

Tens of thousands at a large sports stadium in Cusco, Peru, had their eyes fixed on giant screens, hoping the old prophecies of the Incan shamans would now be fulfilled.

A community center near Jackson, Mississippi, in the United States was crowded with people from all walks of life, ready to see whoever it was that would soon appear.

In all these locales, the dissonance of some nearby refusing to watch the event and feeling angry or threatened was understood yet ignored. Clearly, it took a distressed humanity still reeling with chaos, calamities, and conflict, yet alive with hope and expectancy, to create this vast worldwide audience.

Finally, the moment arrived. Zune sat with Naylu, Tashi, Aiyana, and many folks of the community. They were open to the moment, hoping it would have a stimulus potent enough to begin a new era of cooperation and renewal for humanity.

The world was primed. The guest was ready.

With just a few words, UN Secretary General Ameena Zakuani introduced the unique speaker. He was simply dressed, a man not easily identifiable with any race or culture. His handsome face, seemingly familiar, radiated a kind, powerful presence. Seven Great Ones, recognized by many, stood close by.

As he began to speak, a deep hush of silence pervaded the attentive masses.

Imbued with a luminous, golden glow, the countenance of the Prism was gently riveting. Each listener around the globe heard him in their own language. People felt as if he was speaking directly to them. And he was.

"Friends, I am exceedingly grateful to be with you at this time of humanity's tremendous challenges."

His golden aura grew brighter.

"Know yourselves as part of the One Humanity and the One Universal Life."

Golden light fully enveloped him, his features barely visible.

"On all levels of existence, a new energy is flowing, bringing us nearer to the Source of Life itself."

People felt this Life alive in their hearts.

"Together, we can create a world free from deprivation and war where all may have the basic necessities of life: food, housing, health care, safety."

We can.

"We whom you call Great Ones advise and guide, yet all of us must do the needed work together."

We will.

"My friends, these things are not dreams. All of this will be yours. I am a Prism, through which love and goodwill flows. Feel it. Be it. Use it."

With these final words, a brilliant, rosy, golden ray streamed forth from the Prism and the Great Souls, a stupendous wave, flowing through the hearts of all willing to receive it.

In this moment, all shared the experience of the one and the same energy, connecting us with each other and all life.

In this moment, profound inspiration was felt in the souls of all who opened to it.

In this moment, the world appeared illumined in a light unlike any other.

Across the globe, the heart of humanity began awakening after endless centuries of slumber. A vast reservoir of goodwill flowed forth from the soul of humanity.

As the energy radiating from the Prism slowly subsided, many millions around the world found their way into the streets, parks, communities, and houses of worship, joyful in the awe of their profound shared experience.

Was there a cloud in the sky anywhere? The sun seemed much brighter than usual. People felt so spiritually alive, not yet trying to define the experience via their conventional religious concepts. Many were bewildered by the revealing wonder. Goodwill permeated the atmosphere.

This first dawn of a new era provided a wake-up call so desperately needed, and it was heard. Not quite the Rapture expected by many. No shortcut to Shamballa. Simply an opportunity to live more sensibly, embracing awareness of the interconnectedness of all life. The imperative to act accordingly became evident. Humanity will determine how to do so with some help from Great Souls. After all, zeal is the realization of a necessity.

A few days later, Naylu and Zune got into his car, heading out onto the Infinite Highway of Life. The fiery love filling their hearts is what the experience with the Prism was really all about. Slowly driving up into the mountains above Transcendent Valley, ready to serve, they knew their destination will be evident when they arrive.

Forever to know the universe itself as a road,
as many roads, as roads for traveling souls,
alive, forever forward…

ABOUT THE AUTHOR

Bradley Berg is a practical, visionary idealist residing in rural New York. He is deeply rooted in life's esoteric foundations. Bradley organizes conferences on peacebuilding, leadership, environmental issues and more, as a board member of a local nonprofit. Bradley has explored remote Tibet, hitchhiked across the US, and managed a natural foods, wholesale cooperative. He spent decades working in the mental health field and has a degree in Chemistry. Family, music, nature, current events, friends, goodwill, and group work are integral to his life. Bradley strives to "Shine the Light."